Hope in Anarchy

Kyuka Lilymjok

ISBN 978 978 069 1707

Published by:
Free Pen Publishers
10 Lachlan Close, Maitama, Abuja

Any people depicted in stock imagery provided by Thinkstock are models, and such images are being used for such purposes only.

This book is printed on acid-free paper.

The views expressed in this work are solely those of the author and do not necessarily reflect the views of the publisher. The publisher hereby disclaims any responsibility for them.

To my wife Maria, and my children: Justice,
Sunfair and Fairprincess

Order is a trick authority has sold to the poor
When the poor find the lie in order
They will return it to the seller with a sword

Chapter One

Ahoka stretched, turned and gradually sat up under the bridge. He was a tall, fair complexioned boy always wearing a brooding expression on his face. Asabeni bridge located between Desowa and Beku Island had become his only home since the day he and his father were thrown out of their one-room apartment in Desowa because they could not pay the three thousand rida monthly rent demanded by their landlord.

Sitting under the bridge, he threw a pitiful glance at his father sleeping on his back near him. He had just returned from Beku Island where he worked as a watchman in one of its magnificent villas. Whenever he returned from work in the morning, he would throw his big stick into the tall grass that in a providential way served as walls to this house without walls. Without asking him how he had passed the night, he would drop down on his back and almost immediately drift into a snoring sleep. He sometimes wondered if his father did not sleep on his feet on his way home. If not, he must have been carrying sleep in one of the big pockets of his faded jacket, which he rubbed on his face the moment his back hit the floor of the bridge. And he had this snoring habit that always irritated and tasked his nerves. Most days, it was his nasal strains that told him he was back from work. It was as if it had turned into his alarm bell.

However, under this irritation was a seething envy of his father's ability to sleep so soundly on the hard floor of the bridge with motorists honking and blaring their horns during the early morning rush in beat the nerve-racking and patience-sapping Beku traffic. Though the bridge had been his home for years now, he never seemed to get used to it. The baked hand of hospitality which the bridge had extended to them and which his father appeared to have accepted, he seemed eternally, to be hopelessly out of its reach. Even on a good night when the urge to sleep was strong in him, he could not sleep for more than five hours. Then he would wake up with his ribs aching and big mosquitoes buzzing round his ears like an army of migrating bees. The mosquitoes were always a greater menace than the hard floor. During their season, and in their house under the bridge close to Asabeni lagoon, it meant all the year through, they knew neither night nor day. Every time was feasting time for them and he was their meal. Even when they had a mosquito net on, the mosquitoes had a way of getting through the net to suck them. Whenever he killed a mosquito and saw his palms stained with blood he knew too well to be his, he would beat his hand on the floor of the bridge and rail like a mad man. Though his father and Ojoro another destitute living under the bridge with them often caught fish in the lagoon particularly at night, this was not enough to make up for the horror of living under the bridge. Indeed, whatever they got from the fish, he believed the mosquitoes took away more from their bodies.

Further east of where he was sitting was the mat Ojoro slept on and the mosquito net that secured him from the vicious mosquitoes of Asabeni bridge. Ojoro was by the lagoon inspecting his fish traps. From there, he would go out and only return late in the evening. Not often was he to be found under the bridge in the day time. Though they met him on the same side of the bridge when they first came to live under it, they did not know where he spent his days. He was a very quiet man that took care not to involve himself with anybody either for good or for ill. The whole day he would be away returning to the bridge late in the evening only to pass the night.

Again, Ahoka peeked at his father, then looked away into the nearby bush. His eyes fell on the big stick lying in the tall grass. Anytime he saw that stick, he wondered how his father could keep armed robbers at bay using such a stick as his only weapon. He had heard of the dare-devilry with which armed robbers in Beku operate with their self-loading rifles and General Purpose Machine Guns. How then could a watchman hold his own against such armed robbers using a mere stick? He always felt that his father was merely throwing away his life by not insisting that Okime his master provide him with a gun, moreso that he served as an artillery soldier in the Wajuwan war of salvation and therefore very much at home with the use of fire arms. But his father always said he has tried his best to make Okime his master see why he should have a gun but to no avail. One day while they were eating *eba* under their bridge residence, he broached the topic again. His father stopped eating and began washing his hands in a small bowl of water dotted with small lakes of palm oil.

'You think say I wan die like cockroach?' he asked, rubbing his hands with a dirty rag. 'I tell you I don ask my Ogar many times say make him gif me him small automatic gun, but Ogar no gree.'

'So, e get gun?' he asked, pausing in his eating to stare open-mouthed at his father.

'My pikin, which big man no get gun for dis Beku? Even sef, no be one gun dem get. Dem get one for house and one for dem cars.'

'Why him no wan give you one of him guns then?' he asked, surprised.

'My pikin, you never sabi dis big men dem,' his father said, laying back on the floor of the bridge to scratch where an insect had bitten him. 'Dem selfish well, well. Dem only wori na how to protect dem lives and dem pikins. Dem no know say poor man get life wey him wan protect too.'

'But him no know say if e gif you gun na dat time you go fit protectam well?' he asked, a confused expression replacing the surprise on his face.

'My pikin, I say you never sabi dis big men,' his father said, releasing a belch that stank of palm oil. 'Dem no dey think like we. Dem thinking be say. God create poor man first to dey serve them, second to protect them, lastly to think of himself. So poor man no suppose think of himself but him Ogar, and e must do anything to protectam whether or not Ogar give am the thing wey e go take protectam. If they killam while protecting Ogar, then Ogar must have something to protect himself. Dat is how dem dey think my pikin. Not like poor man wey dey see him neighbour like human being too.'

'Papa, na wa o for poor man,' he said, mournfully.

'No be small wahala my pikin, na big wahala,' his father said, standing up to chase a polythene bag that has been blown by the wind from their colony into the nearby bush.

'Rich man na funny man.'

'Who talkam my pikin? Rich men, na craze men. The funny thing for dem thinking be say even as dem expect poor man to protect them, dem no go trustam with gun. Dem dey fear say one day e go kill them with the gun wey dem giveam. Na mumu people, if you no know.'

Since that day, he had not mentioned the issue again to his father. But the fear for his life still haunted him. This fear doubled in intensity whenever it was 7am and he was not yet back from work.

Sitting under the bridge now, thoughts of the ill treatment his father was receiving in Okime's house and the risks he was running everyday of his stay in that house tormented his mind with an intensity he rarely experienced. He made to stand up to fetch the stick from the bush, but slipped and fell down hitting his mouth on the floor. Hot tears came cascading down his cheeks as he felt his mouth with his hand. He could not imagine what could be more harrowing than being a resident of a bridge with a slanting floor, acute insecurity arid grave inconveniences as bedmates. They slept, ate and bathed in these inconveniences. They went out and came back to be welcomed by them.

His weeping like a punctual mosquito gradually bored into his father's sleep and he opened his eyes.

'Wetin you dey cry Ahoka?' he grunted, blinking his eyes with a deliberate rapidity strange for one just waking up from sleep.

"I wan stand up, naim I come nack my head for bridge, naim I come fall down,' he sobbed.

'Wetin dat mean?' his father flared up. 'Na today you first sleep for under dis bridge? I beg 1 no wan hear you disturb my sleep again,' he said and turned to face the other side. 'I don forget sef,' he went on after a short interval, 'you no go go work today?'

'I go go o,' he said, running out of the bridge towards the lagoon. Somehow he had forgotten that today like any other day since he was thrown out of school because his father could not pay the seven thousand rida demanded by the school authority pursuant to the newly introduced Book Policy in all post primary institutions in the Republic, he had to comb the streets of Beku in search of discarded empty bottles, plastic cans and rusty iron bars for sale to bottling companies and steel rolling mills.

When he reached the lagoon, he slipped out of his clothes and took a long dive. When he had swam a considerable distance into the lagoon, he turned and started swimming back to shore. At the shore, he rubbed his body with a small piece of soap and splashed water on his body to wash off the foam. He put on his clothes and got back to the bridge to be greeted by his father's unnerving nasal strains. Quietly, he picked up his empty fertilizer sack and slunk away leaving his father dead to the world.

Chapter Two

On the road, Ahoka did not know whether to go to Voro, Beku Island or Desowa. This was the difficult choice he was faced with every day. Beku Island and Voro were residential areas for sharks as rich men were called in Beku. If your monthly income did not fall within the six figures income earners you could not dream of taking up accommodation in either of these areas. In either of these areas, he was sure of having a field day and returning home with a lot of bottles and plastic cans as there would be few children competing with him for these wares. But the problem with these areas was the nagging fear that always accompanied him whenever he was in either of them. The rich living in these areas saw any poor man that moved close to their houses as a thief and they did not hide their suspicion and anger. The hostile expressions on their faces and the growling dogs that lurked behind their fences always made his hair stand on end. One day while he was ferreting for bottles and plastic cans in a refuse receptacle in Voro, a rich man with a paunch that made walking herculean barked at him to tell him what he was hanging around his fence for.

'Ogar, I am looking for bottles,' he said with a sinking heart.

'You children of wretches!' the man bellowed, stubbing out the dead end of his cigar. 'Can't you ever think of other places to ferret for your bottles other than this neighbourhood? I mean there are too many flies around here without you adding to them.' With that, he walked to his house. When he reached his garage, he turned and saw him still standing by the gate. 'So you won't beat it?' he shouted, pointing at him. 'If I come out and find you still standing there, you will have to explain to my dog what you are nosing around for.'

He immediately picked the bottles and plastic cans in his sack and fled back home crying. For three weeks he did not go back to Voro. And when he did eventually, he made sure he steered clear of the fences, not only because of the lurking dogs, but because he had also heard that the sharks had started electrifying their fences and one might get electrocuted the moment one comes into contact with any of them.

But if he went to Desowa, he would be free of all these fears because only the poor lived there, and flies seldom chase flies. But then, he would return home with fewer bottles as there would be other children also scrambling for them. It was this kind of dilemma that sometimes made him go to Hacul beach to fetch sea water for people who needed it for medicinal purposes or for making charms. In fact, he would have preferred this trade to scratching the streets for empty bottles if not that it had its own hazards too. He might spend the whole day at the beach without a single soul to buy his water. Most sick people who needed the water to cure their ailments preferred to come to the beach to be treated there by any of the native doctors that thronged the beach plying their trade. These native doctors known as *Bekoda* in Beku were to be found at the beach day and night.

One day, he was at the beach and there was this old man brought to the beach by his son for treatment by a *Bekoda*. The man by the way he was walking was probably suffering from rheumatism. He was stripped from his head to his toes. Only a loincloth wrapped round his waist interfered with his nudity. The *Bekoda* that was to treat him with the sea water was a young, tall man also stripped from head to toes with only short knee breeches breaking his nudity. He held the patient by his waist and walked him into the waves that surged inland only to roll back to sea. They stopped where the weaves would always bathe the old man's knees before rolling back. The *Bekoda* started his incantations in a sing-song chant. The language of the incantations was esoteric meant only for the ears of the *Bekoda* and the water spirits he was communing with. Now and then, he bent down and scooped some of the sea water with his right hand and massaged different parts of the patient's body with it. Sometimes he left the patient and walked farther into the sea. Then his voice rose higher and his hands thrust forward and backward as if he were sending the water spirits to the patient behind him. Ahoka who stood watching him, at a point started wondering who was sick between the *Bekoda* and his patient.

Today, he was on the brink of deciding to go to Hacul beach when he sighed and began walking in the direction of Voro. There was one particular street in Voro where he usually found a lot of empty bottles. Any day he was in Voro for work, that street was always the first that he traced from beginning to end. On a lucky day, after tracing the street, he would have collected enough bottles and he would go back home from there.

This was Buwani Street. It ran along the lagoon and curved into Voro proper by a big palm tree standing on the shore of the lagoon. Apart from providing him with bottles, he also liked the street because running along a waterfront; he could easily find a place to rest his tired feet without attracting the suspicion and hostility of the rich'.

But for no reason he did not feel like going to that street this morning; instead, he headed for Landscape Avenue. He had been on this street only three times and each time he did not like the chilling silence that pervaded the street. Though there was always no sign of life on the street, he always had a sneaky feeling of being watched behind doors. The street always reminded him of the small cemetery between Voro and Beku Island where he used to hear the footsteps of someone following him on his heels, but when he looked back, he would see nobody. The only time he saw life on the street was when a fat woman with ruddy cheeks, obviously a woman of comfortable circumstances, climbed into a Mercedes Benz car and drove away with the fury of a plane taking off.

Today when he arrived the street, he saw the same woman standing by her garage door, her hands folded on her chest and a vapour of sadness clouding her face. It was clear she was sorrowing over something pretty bad. 'What could be the problem of a person living in this area with its smashing buildings and well kept surroundings?' he wondered. Certainly not mosquitoes that were sucking away their lives under the bridge. He stood near the refuse can of her house at the gate looking at her afraid that any moment she might look towards the gate and catch him prying on her. Suddenly, one of her children about the same age with him opened the sitting room door and ran towards her.

'Mummy, mummy, I want to drink tea,' he whined. When he reached her, she hugged him affectionately saying, 'Sebimi, you want to drink tea? But you know I don't prepare your breakfast. Go and meet the cook. Tell him to prepare tea for you and don't forget to add butter to your bread, you hear?' she said, releasing the boy from her arms. 'Also, he should pour a lot of milk into your tea,' she added as the boy ran back into the house. 'See how my children are drying up,' she lamented, the sad expression coming back to her face.

Tears came to Ahoka's eyes as he stood watching this scene of love and filial affection between the fat woman and her child. This was a boy about the same age with him; yet the only thing they had in common was that they were both human beings breathing life. There the similarities ended and the differences began. He bent down and started removing all the empty bottles in the garbage can into his sack. At the bottom of the can *was* a ragbag. Without thinking, he picked it up and dropped it into his sack; then he picked up the sack onto his shoulder and moved on leaving the fat woman still standing by the garage door. As he walked away from the house, tears welled up in his eyes.

'Which time will I too know the love of a mother?' he cried. 'And when will I live in this kind of house drinking tea and sleeping my life away?'

Chapter Three

Ahoka's problems started the day Solo his father received his army discharge gratuity. For three years, he had gone to the army legion office in Beku almost begging that he be paid his gratuity of four hundred thousand rida. But he always returned home with a baleful story of a corrupt bureaucratic bottleneck that was denying him his gratuity. Finally, he was paid after backhanding the pension officer and the desk clerk who on all occasions previous to his payment, had always looked at him with the condescending air of a man of superior means, but on the day of his payment had looked at him like a dog eyeing a fat bone. It was evening, so he hurried back home for fear of running into one of the armed robbery bandits infesting Beku. When he got home, he went straight to his big iron box and put the money inside. Sometime towards mid night, his wife started tapping him telling him to wake up and hear the creaking of their door. But he slept on with the usual nasal strains. She had to squeeze his nose before he could wake up.

'Wetin now?' he grunted still smarting under the urge to sleep on. 'Why you dey wake me for dis time of the night wey man pikin never see sleep, sleep well?'

'Listen,' she said, 'I think I can hear small, small noise for outside.'

'Dis woman you no dey well at all, at all,' he said, laying back. 'If you dey hear noise for outside nko; wetin dat noise take concern man pikin sleeping for him room?'

'But papa Ahoka, na for our domot the noise dey comot,' she said with a tinge of hysteria. 'E be like say some people wan open our door for force.

On his wife saying this, all the sleep in Solo vanished. For the past twelve years that they had lived together as husband and wife, he had come to respect his wife's uncanny instinct for danger. Once, while he was still in the army serving at Kwawe, she had woke him up saying she could hear the movement of something like a snake in their room. He had dismissed her fears as those of a woman and slept on. But no sooner was he asleep than a big python fell off the planks of their roof on top of them on their bed. His wife nearly died of fright and he could only roll down the floor frightened out of his skin. The python crawled over their bodies and slipped out of the room through a big opening between the door and the floor without doing them any harm. Whenever he remembered that incident, he came out in cold sweat.

'You sure say dis noise dey come from our domot?' he asked in a frightened voice.

'If I no sure, I go wake you?'

'Then make I go see wetin wan wake us for dis time of the night when man pikin never see sleep, sleep well, he said, getting off from the bed.

But the wife jumped and drew him back. 'Where you wan go?' she asked in a terrified voice. 'You no know say e fit be armed robbers wey wan break open our door?'

'Armed robbers?' he held his breath, his right hand going to his mouth. Though he had served in the publican army and even fought the Wajuwan war of salvation as an artillery, he still had a lot of water in his stomach especially where armed robbers were involved. Tales of their primitive and cruel methods of operation always turned his stomach round. The gratuity money neatly stacked inside his iron box also did not help matters.

'But wetin man pikin do armed robbers?' he said sheepishly, reaching for his big stick under the bed. He picked it up and stood up. As he took a tottering step towards the door, a loud sound from outside reached them inside the room. It was the unmistakable sound of a violent kick being dealt on their door. But the door held on. Ahoka's mother held her breath in fear then started sobbing. Solo stood in the centre of the room with his big stick frozen with fear.

A second kick sent a splinter of wood flying across the room to land on Ahoka sleeping peacefully by his mother. This second kick seemed to have thawed the paralysis in Solo and he sprang into action. He reached the door in two strides and started wedging it with his big stick by standing one end of the stick on the floor and the other end against the door. Then he ran across the room to pick a big table on which stood a table fan and other items. He did not bother to remove the items in the table but simply withdrew it leaving all items on the table to crash to the floor. But, before he could reach the door, a stocky man drove his shoulder into the door. The door almost came off from the hinges as the man came crashing into the room, gun in hand and a mask on face. Two other men were on his heels also wearing masks with guns in firing position. Their lips were squeezed up into vicious snarls.

'Men, you cover the bullock while I do the talking,' the stocky man said wandering to sit on the only cushion chair in the room. From the way he spoke, it was obvious he was the leader of the robbery gang.

'Sure, we gotta do that right boss,' said his man covering Solo with his gun behind. Solo stood limply by the table while the two men covered him with their guns front and back. Their leader sat on the cushion with the mouth of his rifle pointing at his wife.

During his career in the Republican army, he had come to develop a morbid fear and respect for a gun. He saw it as a small house of death and whoever has command over it, has command over death. If he wants you dead, all he needs do is to touch a small nail in his house of death and you would be dead. As he stood by the table facing the small mouth of the gun, he wondered whether even in his military career, he had been brought closer to death like this. The only time he was put under a similar situation was when a platoon of the Republican army, which he belonged was cut off by the Wajuwan soldiers and shelled down. He was the only man that survived that bombardment and he did so by clutching his stomach with both hands and slumping on the ground like a man that had been shot. But this night, it seemed that trick would not avail him much good. Not with only him being covered back and front by two vicious looking hoodlums. His only route of escape was to slam the table on the man in front of him any moment he was off guard. But what of the man behind him? He would have nailed him before he goes as far as picking the table. He turned to look at the distance between him and the man.

The man took two quick steps towards him and hit him hard on his head with the butt of his rifle. 'Babe,' he hissed, saliva dropping from his mouth. 'You look straight: never look back. You go funny on me, I get rough.'

Solo spread out on the floor unconscious. His wife started wailing bouncing on their string bed.

You shut up your trap or I shut it for you,' the stocky man said, looking mean; 'and when I shut a trap, I shut it for good.'

She stopped crying and sat curled up on the bed like a doll. The stocky man turned and looked at the man who had hit Solo. There was a fiery anger in his eyes.

'Jims, why bash the bullock so hard?' he demanded, his words coming out with a hiss. 'You ain't get any sense at all. If you gotta kill him, why not wait until we grab the dough?'

'You don't blame me boss?' Jims whined in defence. The bloke wantta get at me and I gotta stop him.'

'All right men,' the boss said, waving him to silence. 'You take this joint to bits while I give the broad society; get it?'

'Yes, boss,' the two men answered together and began searching the room with the trained expertise of nosey pigs.

Ahoka who had woken up, stared at the strange men with the horror of a lamb in hyenas' carnival.

When they got to the iron box, they flipped it open and spilled its contents on the floor.

'Men, the bloke sure gets the brass,' Jims cried, when the five hundred rida notes spilled on the floor with other things inside the box.

Ahoka's mother started wailing again.

'Babe, I said shut up!' the boss shouted at her, his finger curling round the trigger of his gun. 'Anything like that again from you and you get it. I ain't taking any shit from a bitch like you,' he went on turning to his men. 'You pick the dough into this bag and we scram,' he said, throwing a small sack at them. 'And you make it snappy. I am getting sick of this pigsty.'

The two men hurriedly packed the money into the sack with the greed of monkey s and stood up.

'All right, let's beat it,' the boss said, getting to his feet.

'What of the dish sitting over there?' Jims asked with a leer.

'What about her?' the boss asked, suspiciously.

'Ain't you see she is a fine dish?' Jims said, the leer on his face expanding.

'So, she is a fine dish; what then?' the boss asked in a hard grating voice.

'What else, but we give her the works,' Jims said in a lewd voice. 'Please, boss, I wantta make her.'

The boss stood looking at him his mind very busy. It was time he got rid of Jims, he told himself. There was hardly any operation they carried out that Jims did not nearly foil with his randy ways. Not that Jims was not useful in other respects. In fact, when it came to being vigilant and tough, he could be counted on to hold his own. But to his mind, these good qualities of Jims were not enough to make up for his obsession with sex. In one of their operations in Beku city, they beat the police only with the skin of their teeth and it was because Jims wanted to have it off with the daughter of their victim. If he allowed him to continue mixing business with pleasure, only God knew the grief they would come to in future. That would be chancing his arm and he was in no mind to run chances. But what was he to do? He knew that of the two men he was operating with. Jims was more dangerous and pulled a gun faster. So, taking him on a one-on-one shooting duel was out of the question. To throw him out would also not work as he would not only ask for an account and a sharing of their hot assets salted away in their hideout, but might even seek to square up scores with him. And to the small mind of an unscrupulous creep like Jims, squaring up scores meant shoving a whiff of bullets into his guts. From the look of things, it appeared his greatest weapon against Jims was surprise. This he would employ to his maximum advantage when Jims was under the firm grip of his weakness: sex.

'All right Jims, you can have your pleasure,' he said in a very casual voice.' We will wait for you outside.'

If Jims was not consumed by lust that raged through his debauched body like a drunken fellow, he would have spotted that his boss was too polite to mean well. But as it were, he could only see and think one thing: the woman sitting curled up on the bed. He dropped his gun on the floor and undid his trousers. Then he started advancing on Ahoka's mother, his eyes shut.

Ahoka's mother started screaming, grabbing anything within her reach and hurling them at him.

'Come on babe, shed off your clothes,' he said in a drunken voice. 'Let's play ball. Why cry, babe? You virgin Mary? I ain't gona hurt you babe. Only the works babe, and you gona like it; real works from a real man babe.' Suddenly, he lurched forward to grab her, but she jumped backward and he fell on top of the bed.

'All right babe; if you wantta prove tough, I gona show you I ain't cotton material,' he said, leaping at her.

The boss standing on the doorway fired two quick shots at him and disappeared into the dark night.

The bullets rammed into the back of his head and he folded up like a rag with only a tiny groan.

Chapter Four

Solo did not come to until around 3.30 am. He looked round the room and saw a man lying face down near the bed. There were bloodstains at the back of his head. To his right, stood his wife, her face swollen with weeping. He was not sure he was in his room.

When the armed robbers fled his room after taking his money and killing one of their number, his wife wailed and wailed for help but none came. In Beku, people did not answer such calls for fear of falling victim to the sharp shooting hoodlums. Seeing no help was coming, she attempted bringing her husband to, but he was too far gone to come to that soon. She left him and went to lift the dead body of the hoodlum, but it was too heavy for her to even shift. Even if she could lift it, what would she have done with it? she wondered. She shrugged her shoulders and went to weep by one corner of the room.

'Where we dey?' Solo asked in a croaked voice.

"We dey inside our room,' she said, her throat sore with weeping. 'But we dey insiram without our money.'

'Wetin you say Mama Ahoka?' Solo cried. 'So dem carry our money go? God, wetin your pikin do you wey you wan punisham so, ehn?'

'Papa Ahoka no be only tif dem tif o. Dem also kill dem broda comot leave the dead bodi for we to buryam.'

'You mean say the man lying there na dead bodi?' Solo asked, horrified.

She nodded her head.

'Na dem killam?' he asked, stupidly.

'No, not be them, na you,' she said and hissed.

'Where the man from come?'

'Na one of them.'

'Then why dem come killam?'

'Na the thing wey hard me understand be dat,' she said, her eyes fixed on the dead body. 'But dem killam wey him dey wan chop wetin you chop I come born Ahoka. E be like say their leader no like the thing wey e wan do.'

''Wetin?' Solo asked, startled. 'Dis one, na real baboon pikin. Him mind dirty pass bola. Na God catcham.'

'But, even if na God catcham, why him no catcham for another place, but inside our room?' she said. 'We no get money, we come get dead bodi, which kind wahala be dat?'

'Na my money I dey cry for, not dead bodi wey wan nack my wife. Make e lie rotten there; wetin be my own for inside?'

'Why you dey talk like twelve months pikin?' she said, looking into his eyes. 'Dead bodi dey inside your room and you dey talk say wetin be your own for inside. If police come, you go know say your own dey inside yangfu, yangfu.'

'Police!' he said, rising stiffly to his feet, 'Police.' He had always seen the police as a bunch of troublesome crooks, very good at making trouble but bad at solving it. To him, they are lazy bones that would gladly hang their trouble on your neck at the slightest temptation. He was sure if they find the dead body inside his room, nothing would suit them better than slamming a murder charge on him and make it stick. The armed robbers would give them part of his money and they would mess him up. But what to do with the body had him licked. For a moment, he was tempted to call in the police and hope they would reason like human beings and not charge him with the murder of the man. But he resisted the temptation when he remembered what happened to his friend Bhoboro in the hands of the police.

Bhoboro woke up one morning to find his room burgled and an expensive wristwatch lying under his table. It was obviously left behind in his room by the burglars. The wristwatch turned out to be a stolen property belonging to a Lebanese who had earlier reported its theft to the police. When Bhoboro called at the police station to report the burglary incident and to hand over the wristwatch as an item left behind by the burglars, the police snapped handcuffs on him saying he stole the wristwatch and dismissed his complaint as the tall story of a thief that has developed cold feet following their intensive investigation for the stolen watch. Though he was later released, he came home with a woeful tale of his sojourn in police custody. As for his stolen property, the police were yet to come out with a statement on the theft.

This bitter experience of his friend was still fresh in his mind. The Republican police that he knew would ask him how armed robbers that came to rob him would kill one of their own and leave the corpse in his room. They would collect bribe from the armed robbers and persecute him for murder if they cannot prosecute him. That meant he would be in police custody for a long time; that is, if he did not die from the torture they would subject him to in order to get him confess the crime. What was more, he was in an unfriendly neighbourhood where every man cared only for his own welfare and so he might not get a single soul to testify to having heard gunshots and screams that night. Without such witness, he would be left with only his own words and those of his wife both interested parties. From his knowledge of the Republican police, he saw little cheer in that kind of story.

'Make we go call police o,' his wife said, moving near him. 'We no go sit down here the whole night looking dis dead bodi dey decay dey go.'

'Go call wetin?' he said, blocking his eardrums with his fingers. 'I beg, mama Ahoka make you no mention dat word for my ears again. Police? Dem go ask us wetin we carry and if dem come see say na dead bodi we dey carry, our own don pafuka be dat, unless we fit give them *kola* and where the *kola* dey for dis room?'

'Then wetin you wan make we do?' she asked, her hands wrapped together behind her head.

'If we get small sense,' he said, 'the thing to do na to carry the dead bodi throwey for lagoon dis night.

'Me, I no like dis your sense o,' the wife cried, shaking her head.

'Then make you tell me your own sense make I see if I likeam.'

'My own sense be say make we go call police. No be them gofmen say make dem dey quench dis kind wahala?'

'The thing wey gofmen tell them to dey do na one thing, the thing wey dem dey do na another thing and the two no come be the same thing. Shebi you dey see the sense wey I dey talk?'

'Me I no understand o,' she cried, stamping her feet. 'The only thing wey I know be say make we go call police.'

'For the last time I go tell you make you no mention police for my ears,' he warned her, anger burning in his eyes. 'If you refuse and go call them, you no go come meet me for house. Then you go sit down tell them your tori. May be they go believe you as you be woman. But before you go, try remember wetin happen to our friend Bhoboro for police hand.'

Ahoka's mother did not say anything neither did she go to the police. Together, they dragged the dead man into their wheelbarrow after so much sweat; then Solo began his long and dangerous journey to the lagoon. The body had become very heavy and he was able push it only because the small path he took was devoid of sand and sloped towards the lagoon. All the way, he was on the lookout for trouble. For a good part of his journey, he saw no one and met no one. But down near the lagoon, the figure of a man suddenly sprang up in front of him. He stopped walking, fear making him feel weak at the knees. Should he tip the dead body into the bush where it would certainly be discovered by day break and then run for his dear life or should he wait until the path was clear once more before proceeding to deposit it in the lagoon? If he picked the first option, there was the risk of the dead body being traced to his room somehow. He knew nothing pleased the Republican police like terrorising blighted neighbourhoods like his where they once said crime grows like grass in the forest. If they found the dead body in his neighbourhood, they would terrorise the entire neighbourhood with a view of extorting money from its poor residents. This would make those who heard the commotion around his room to point in his direction and once he has the police in his room, he either settles them or he would have a very rough time in their custody. He experienced a violent jolt in his chest, then a tear of sweat dropped off his face. But if he was able to dump the dead body in the lagoon, it might never be discovered, and if discovered, it would be so far removed from his neighbourhood that any police investigation would be around the lagoon or the neighbourhood where it was found. This meant he should remain standing where he was and wait for a clear passage to the lagoon. But what if some nosey fellow comes along, wouldn't he be worse off than throwing the body into the bush now and risk its being traced to his room? He was in a quandary.

The man moved on quietly towards the lagoon then abruptly turned and started walking back. Solo did not even realise he was coming back until he was right on him.

'Hey man, wetin you dey tanda dey do for darkness?' the man asked in a husky voice trying to make out his face in the darkness.

'Wetin be your own for wetin I dey do for darkness?' he managed to say in a croaked voice.

'Plenty my broda, plenty. How I sure say no be people like you wey dey come tif my fish for night, ehn? Even sef, wetin you dey push for wheelbarrow so?' the man said, peering at the dead body covered with a rag. He pulled out his hand to feel the content of the wheelbarrow.

'OK, broda, I no dey carry your fish; you go leave me alone?' Solo said, holding the man's hand. 'You no see say na the lagoon I dey go so?

How I go carry your fish?' he went on in a voice he could hardly recognise as his.

'If you know say you no dey carry my fish, why you no wan make 1 see wetin you dey carry?' the man said pushing his hand down.

Although Solo was not a man you could exactly describe as strong, he had a wild temper that sometimes drove him to do things a strong man might shrink from. Once under that temper, he had beaten a man and thrown him into a well. Now as he struggled to take the man's hand from the wheelbarrow, that temper took charge of him. He suddenly went limp and came up with an uppercut that shattered the man's lower jaw. The man went out like a snapped torchlight. Solo shove him into the bush and continued hastily with his journey to the lagoon. He entered the lagoon with the wheelbarrow until the water came to his waist, then he tipped the corpse over and came out with the wheelbarrow. His Journey back home was a lot better. He saw no one and met no one.

Chapter Five

Alter the robbers' smash-up, Ahoka and his father stayed in Desowa for only two months and had to leave for the bridge as they could not find the three thousand rida demanded by their landlord as rent. After the robbery, Ahoka's father roamed the streets of Beku scouting for a job, but found none. After about six weeks of intensive search to no good, he was exhausted and out of spirits. Picking a job in the Republic was like picking emeralds in a hay field; though the Republic was supposed to be the barn of Africa; at least so her President had said. Without money and a job, even keeping the wolves from their doorsteps became onerous, not to talk of picking the tabs for their accommodation. So Ahoka and his father had to move out of their one room apartment to live under one of the bridges between Desowa and Beku Island: the Asabeni bridge.

Ahoka's mother was heavy with child and her brother who also lived in Desowa in a one room apartment with his family of seven people, begged Ahoka's father that his sister be allowed to stay behind with him until she was delivered of her baby as she could not cope with the hardship of bridge life toiling with pregnancy. Solo saw sense with him. So only he and Ahoka moved to the bridge with their few belongings. Ahoka would never forget the tears of his mother as he and his father moved off for the bridge leaving her behind.

'Wetin dey make mama cry?' he asked, looking up pleadingly at his father.

'You no go fit understand my pikin,' his father said, fighting hard to hold back the tears that shone in his eyes.

'Shebi na hunger dey woryam?' he ventured again, pulling one of his father's fingers.

'Yes,' Solo said to put pay to the irksome questions of his son.

'But, papa, no be just now wey we chop *Santana* witham?'

Solo did not say anything. Instead, he started dragging him by his hand saying, 'Ahoka, come make we go o. The place wey we dey go dey far o.'

Then he started crying and shouting, 'me I no dey go, if mama no dey go o!'

Everybody that saw and knew what was happening shed tears of sympathy.

Their first night under the bridge was everything horrendous, nothing short of a nightmare. There were the buzzing and sucking mosquitoes, the hard floor of the bridge, the noisy traffic overhead and the biting morning cold to contend with. Ahoka woke up the following morning to find his body covered with rashes where mosquitoes had bitten him. His father was bending down by the lagoon washing his face.

'Papa, Papa!' he cried, running to him. 'See where mosquitoes chop me,' he said, holding out his little hand for his father to see. 'Papa, why we no sleep for Desowa, we come sleep here where mosquito wan chop our bodi finish?'

His father bent down to splash water on his face to hide the tears that came coursing down his cheeks.

'The mosquitoes my pikin?' he said, turning round to hug him. 'Make you no wori.' Today, I go buy mosquito coil as I dey come back from Beku Island. If I lightam, you no go hear one mosquito again my pikin. So make you no wori, you hear?' he said, cuddling him.

'But, papa, what of the cold, what of the hard floor wey we sleep on; shebi mosquito coil go drive all of them comot?'

Solo did not say anything. He had always seen his son as a hardheaded boy. He said things his age mates could never dream of saying. May be he has taken after his mother, he always thought. He knew he was far from being bright even in his elementary days. How could he tell the boy that their only mattress would remain in Desowa for a long time for the use of his pregnant mother; and that for an equally long period, they would have to make do with the hard floor of the bridge unless they ran into some largesse and that was a forlorn hope. Together they walked back to the bridge.

Solo was in the mind of going to Beku Island to hunt for a job as usual, but was at a loss on what to do with little Ahoka. Though Ojoro was on the same side of the bridge with him and there were other destitutes on the other side of the bridge, he could not leave Ahoka alone with them under the bridge, not knowing who they were. Neither could he take him to his mother in Desowa only to go back later to fetch him. To leave him under the bridge would be most unfatherly and he would have only himself to blame for whatever befalls him in his absence. To take him to his mother only to go back later to fetch him would mean his having to be an actor again in the heart-rending drama that was enacted in front of his in-law's house the previous day. For anything, he would avoid that. Only one option remained open to him: that of walking the streets of Beku Island together with his son. He picked it.

They wandered from street to street looking for a job advert, but saw nothing until they came to Fariche street. Fariche street, like any other street in Beku Island, exuded an aura of wealth and class. It also had the singular privilege of having within its stretch a cellar which operated as a social club called *Club de Gallery Human de Vampirists* with membership drawn only from the rich and powerful. At least, so it was rumoured among the poor people. It was in that club, so went the rumour, that the rich met to exhort one another on the need to maintain distance between themselves and the poor as familiarity breeds contempt and even rebellion in the extreme. But more importantly, the club was said to provide a forum for the rich to know themselves for purposes of fairer treatment or assistance in times of need.

Even the President of the Republic was said to be a member of the club and visited it at least once a week under the cover of the night. The fact that the street was the most beautiful both in terms of houses and the trimming of flowers that lined it, lent credence to these rumours.

When Ahoka and his father came to the street, a very big house that looked more like a merchant bank than a residential building attracted their attention. The house plastered with marble was shining like a chip of diamond in the sun. As one passed by its frontage, he was picked up by the gleaming glass doors and windows. On top of it, it was rumoured, sat a man in a watchtower twenty-four hours of the day. He had glued to his eyes a telescopic sight that picked up anything that came within one killometre radius of the house. The house was popularly known in Beku city as 'the Emperor's castle.' There were few houses like it in the whole of Africa south of the Sahara.

By the small culvert that linked the house to Fariche street was the inscription in capital letters: THE OKIMES (OIL MERCHANTS WEST OF THE KORGA). Further down the court leading to the house stood a small signboard with this advert: WATCHMAN WANTED! APPLYWITHIN.

Ahoka and his father stood looking at the house bereft of words. In solo's mind, there could be no question of a man living in this kind of house thinking of going to an imaginary place called heaven. This house was his perfect idea of heaven.

If there was another heaven beyond the clouds, it was for people like him living in hell here on earth. As he looked at the house, his eyes kept returning to the small signboard by the gate. For a long time, they stood under the scorching Beku sun looking at the house but not seeming to see it. At last, Ahoka asked his father, 'papa who get dis fine house?'

"I no know my pikin,' he said, mopping his face with a ragged handkerchief.

"Papa, why you no build us dis kind house?[7] the son asked again, looking up anxiously at the father.

'I no get money my pikin. Na big, big money dem take build dis house. Even sef,' Solo continued after a momentary pause; 'the small money wey I get, wey I for take build us mud house, thieves come tif am, wetin man pikin go do?'

'But, papa, na for where dem come get the plenty money wey dem take build fine house like dis?'

'My pikin, how I go know? The only thing I know be say most of the big men wey get houses for dis Beku Island na army Generals wey don retire and old politicians dem. Dem no straight at all, at all. So dem no go tell you how dem get their money. Some go tell you say na dem salary wey dem take do business and the business come bring plenty, plenty money. Some no go even gree say dem get money even as you dey seeyam for dem hands. You see how dem never straight? Na real mumu people dem be. Dem dey think say poor

36

man no get sense wey e come be say na dem wey no get sense. If monkey sit down dey chop bananas for my farm and e come tell me say e never taste bananas for him life, who be fool?'

'But, papa, I think say you dey army before, why you no come get money?'

'My pikin, I dey army so, so o. But the thing wey come dey army be say na monkey dey work baboon dey chop.'

'Papa wetin dat mean?'

'You no go understand my pikin. Make we begin throwey leg reach dis house see who dey inside.' He started towards the house. Ahoka followed him.

'Papa, who you know for the house?' Ahoka asked as they drew near the gate.' Or na here mama dey?'

'No be here,' his father said, coming to rest by the gate. 'Your mama dey Desowa now. Na because of the thing wey dem write put for dat small signboard we don pass I wan see the owner of the house.'

'Wetin dem write put for the signboard papa?'

'Dem say, they wan gateman wey go dey guard the house.'

'I see,' Ahoka said, inclining his small head to one side. 'But papa, to know book good o,' he went on after a brief pause. 'Papa, shebi you go put me for primary school dis year, because I don dey see Danti wey you say dem born us for the same day dey go primary school?'

'Make you no wori my pikin; I go surely put you for primary school dis year even if we no go chop.'

'O papa! But papa, why person wey get fine place like dis, no pay police to dey guard him house?'

'Dem no trust police,' his father replied. 'Two years ago, one of them wey be Gofnor for Gasho State said since police don fail the state, dem go hire armed robbers to protect the rich of the state.'

'Papa, na wa o.'

'No be small wahala my pikin.'

Chapter Six

After standing at the gate for about three minutes without anybody poking his head to demand what they were hanging around for, Ahoka's father slightly shook the gate and waited.

Within seconds, an out-at- the- elbow looking man appeared from the small cabin by the gate. He was wearing a worn-to-a-shadow safari suit covered with patches. He was the watchman. He has been lying down inside the cabin transported to another world in a reverie. In his reverie, he was the watchman in Club de Gallery Human de Vampirists and the President of the Republic had paid him a visit in his house bringing along a big box of money as gift for his loyalty in not disclosing the President frequents that club. He prostrated on the floor and collected the money from the President. He used the money to build another emperor's castle like that of his master Okime. Sitting on a swivelling chair, he was barking orders at his servants and smiling to himself when he heard the gate being shaken.

He stood inside the gate looking at Ahoka and his father, anger nearly choking him. Why should he wake up from such a sweet dream only to be confronted with these species of human debasement, these wandering Jews? he thought, angrily.

'Wetin, una come do here?' he asked in a voice that left nothing of the anger and contempt he felt for Ahoka and his father.

Ahoka's father looked at him hopping mad. He had always felt like sticking a knife into the shrunken bellies of poor men who instead of having fellow feelings for fellow poor men, chose to fly in their faces simply because they had the unenviable privilege of eating the faeces of the rich. Standing before this down-at-a-heel looking man, he felt like spitting on his face.

'If na you be dog for dis house, you no sabi bark well,' he said, clenching and unclenching his fists.

The man quickly opened the gate and took a careless swing at Ahoka's father. Solo parried his blow and landed two quick solid punches on the man's belly. The horn-mad star-gazer was not cut out for this kind of punches and he spread out on the ground groaning in pain.

Solo stood looking at him boiling with anger. Somewhere in the main house a door opened and closed. Some minutes later the front door opened and a podgy, light complexioned looking man stepped out onto the terrace. He started waddling towards the gate as fast as his short legs could carry him. He kept blinking his eyes as if the sunrays were offensive to him. The stargazer and his watchman saw him coming and quickly got up trying unsuccessfully to put on a more dignified appearance.

Solo watched the podgy man coming still looking angry and unrepentant. When he got to the gate, his watchman curtsied in greeting with his knee nearly touching the ground. Then he went to stand by his cubicle. His master appeared not to have heard or seen him as he walked to Solo. He stopped about two metres to him and gave him the kind of stare he would a fly that has fallen into his soup. Solo stared back at him still fuming with rage.

'You son of a wretch!' he bawled. 'What has walked you to this part of the city? Don't you know this Island is strictly reserved for the nouveau riche? Oh....' he muttered, slumping his head in utter exhaustion. 'I think time is ripe to make the Presidency insulate us with a legislation barring these naked sons of misery from invading comfort on the Island.'

'But ogar, no be you write dat thing put for gate?' Solo asked, pointing at the small signboard.

'Oh, the signboard?' he said, a somewhat embarrassed expression creeping into his face. 'I nearly forgot about it; are you here in respect of it?'

'Yes, sir,' Solo said.

'In that case, wait for me,' he said, turning to his watchman. He stared at him for a brief moment then said, 'I sometimes wonder if I am not under the spell of a diabolical force to keep a crippled and dumb bloke like you at my gate. Imagine this reedy man taking you in his strides without any sweat.' he went on pointing at Ahoka's father. 'Oyah, go and bring my reclining chair in the sitting-room and place it under that umbrella tree,' he said, turning to Solo.

The watchman fled to the main house tottering here and there but never stopping until he disappeared into the house. Soon he was out with the chair slung on his shoulder. He was on the double again.

On seeing him, his master motioned to Ahoka's father to follow him to the umbrella tree at the centre of the big compound. Solo and his son followed him like abject Shinto devotees.

'Yes, my dear tough man of the Tyson stock; what do you know about being a watchman?' he asked, lounging on his chair.

Ahoka's father told him that he had never been a watchman before, but as an ex-service man, he was sure, he was well equipped and disposed for the job.

'I have no doubt that you are handmade for the job,' the man said, revealing two white teeth in what he called a smile, 'seeing the ease with which you cut the air from Berijo's swollen head. The job is yours.'

'How much you go dey pay me for month end?' Ahoka's father asked when the man appeared not in a hurry to tell him what was his salary for the offered job.

'Six thousand rida,' he said, looking closely at him.

'Six thousand rida,' Solo's face fell to pieces. 'But ogar dat amount dey too small now,' he said, not hiding his disappointment. 'How man and him family go fit live on dat kind money for dis time wey gofmen don bring rida devaluation programme comot the money wey dey inside rida leave ordinary paper wey no fit buy common gari for man pikin?'

'I said six thousand rida and that is the top price. Take it or leave it,' he said with a note of finality. 'Rida has become useless, am I supposed to pay for that?'

'Ogar, I no say make you pay foram,' Solo said, squatting before him. 'But na God I dey take beg you say make you pity me and my pikin plus wife dem pay me seven thousand rida.'

'Should I consider you my watchman on a salary of six thousand rida or do I wait for another man? Of course, you know there are a thousand and one men of the sidewalks who will smile at this offer.'

'OK, ogar, I gree,' he said in a tight, thin voice looking at the ground. 'Which time I go start the work?'

'Tomorrow of course!' The podgy man said, rocking his chair. 'Do you think I put up that signboard for the fun of it? This evening, I will put up a roaster of the shift-order you and Berijo would be guarding the house.'

Ahoka and his father returned home happy that at least, they had gotten something, miserable as it might be-on which to live.

Chapter Seven

Four months after Ahoka and his father left Desowa to live under the bridge, Ahoka's mother was seized by labour of child-bearing. Solo was sent for from Desowa. He went and stayed with her until evening when her labour grew severe. Together with his brother in-law, they carried her into a rickety *kuwa-kuwa* bus running Memu and Desowa. The jolts and sways of the bus as it sped towards Memu nearly made her have a miscarriage on the way. At Memu's last bus stop, they managed to get down even as the bus conductor was already blaring Desowa again. They walked the remaining way to Beku-city General Hospital. When they got to the hospital, Ahoka's mother *was* panting and gasping for breath. She collapsed on a long bench inside the hospital. Her husband approached one of the nurses on duty and drew her attention to the state of his wife. The nurse looked at her sprawled on the bench and looked away without saying anything.

'No be you I dey talk to?' Solo shouted at her, anger fast getting the better of him.

'I hope, you know the new rate for taking a bed in the maternity ward?' she said by way of reply.

'How much e be?' he asked, his heart skipping a beat.

'Eight thousand rida,' she said, tapping the floor with her right foot.

'Eight thousand wetin?' he asked, sweat breaking out on his forehead. 'Abi na una go bom the pikin foram?'

'I said eight thousand rida,' the nurse repeated.

'I hear you,' he said, trying to get a grip of himself.

'Eight thousand rida? Where man pikin go find dat kind money save him wife? Madam, shebi una go fit accept five hundred rida now, then I go sign paper come pay the remaining money for month end?' he asked in despair.

'Accept what?' the nurse asked, laughing. 'This man, I am sure you don't know what you are talking. Don't you know trust has since fled this country and will never return? If we cannot accept such undertaking as you proposed from the sharks of this city, how can we accept it from you?'

When Solo begged and pleaded with her to no avail, he ran back to Beku Island to ask his master for a loan or pay-advance only to be queried as to what he had been doing with his salary.

'But, ogar, you *know* say since dis rida devaluation thing wey gofmen come bring plant for we Republic, rida no come get value again,' he pleaded.

'Rida devaluation or no devaluation,' Okime said, blowing out a stream of rich cigar smoke, 'I have no money to give you. The only money I would have given you, Bemi my first daughter has already requested for her trip to the States. You can talk to her though,' he went on as an afterthought. 'If she would rather you have it; why not, come and have it.'

He left the house then and ran back to Memu. There was no use going to talk to Bemi. Going to her for help was like going to the desert for flowers or trying to squeeze water out of a rock. Of all Okime's children, he knew Bemi to be the sauciest. He would never forget the day she threatened to turn over steaming vegetable oil in a frying pan on his head if he moved near the kitchen again without being invited.

'You stupid, old man!' she had shouted at him. 'Who asked you over here? Why did you come stealing on me as it I were your wife or do you think this is Desowa where decency and privacy have gone down the gutters?'

'Na me you dey curse so?' he said, itching to smack her on her face and hurl her out of the house through the kitchen window. 'You no know say I old reach to born pikin like you? Oh God, my head! Dis world don begin get as e be o. How small pikin go curse old man like me because him no get money?'

'So you won't leave me alone.' she turned and looked at him standing on the threshold of the kitchen. 'Anyway, I don't blame you; you can afford to take all the liberties in the world. After all, daddy doesn't put the domestics in this house where they belong. One of these days, I am quite sure we will wake up to find a quit notice hanging on our door knob issued by one of our own domestics. By the way, what brought you here this time of the night?" she asked, walking towards him with a frying pan in her hand. He stood looking at her trembling with rage. When she got near him, she stopped and peered at him as if he were a reptile that had strayed into her bedroom. 'Is daddy sure this man is not some lunatic?' she said more to herself than to him. 'I think, we should bring in a psychiatrist to examine his coconut head.'

He hissed and left the kitchen without bothering to tell her it was her boyfriend Yoda that had paid her a visit. At the gate, he told Yoda she was not in.

When he arrived the hospital, his wife was dead. She had died from severe bleeding shortly before he came in. According to his brother in-law who he left in the hospital with her, when she started bleeding profusely, the nurses around scampered into different wards to avoid having to speak with her blood that was coming out to plead with them.

Where to bury her became his next headache. The small cemetery between Beku Island and Voro was strictly for the rich. It was called *Monumental Ground of the Ruling spirits*. According to Okime his master, the ground now being used as the cemetery was bought many years ago by a catholic priest from Rome who later donated it to the Blessed People's Church of which Okime was a member. As a matter of fact, only rich people attended the church and so only they had the privilege of being buried there; though they had always maintained anybody could be buried there provided his relations had the money to erect a befitting tomb for him. To erect a befitting tomb there sure cost money. It was a concrete affair from the bottom of the grave to about two feet above sea level. The very rich even had life size statues of their dead relations on their tombs.

Solo knew all these, so he did not consider the cemetery an alternative. But he would not like to bury her near the bridge as the grave would be an open wound in his heart. Neither could he throw her into the lagoon as some people did. What then was he to do with her body in Beku where almost every available space had been taken up by buildings or big signboards threatening court action for trespass in respect of pieces of land yet to come under the tyranny of bricklayers? Finally, he decided to bury her in the bush between Beku and Tiruku. They hired a taxi and sped out of Beku with the body towards Tiruku.

When Ahoka's mother died, her death to him then was more like the temporal loss of food to a teasing visitor against whom he must wail and whimper until it was given back to him. It was far from a permanent separation from her and all its grim consequences. But as the years wore on, the brutal finality of her death began to sink into his mind. Whenever he saw a child about his age in the warm consort of his mother, he would start crying cursing whoever it was that allowed his mother to die leaving him a disconsolate child.

Chapter Eight

After successfully completing primary school at Ronfo Primary School in Desowa, Ahoka proceeded to Semina Government Secondary School located between Desowa and his bridge residence. Right from his primary school days in Ronfo, he was a very bright and diligent student always gracing his poor family background with excellent performances in all class-work and examinations. He was particularly excellent in English language, arithmetic and social studies. Whenever an assignment was given, he rushed home after school hours to soak *gari,* then settled down to work it out diligently. He sat quietly in one comer of the class hardly raising his hand to answer questions thrown to the class by their teachers though he knew the answers. But because most of the teachers knew him as a brilliant pupil, few of them went out of his class satisfied without putting a question or two to him.

But it was in Semina Secondary School that Ahoka shone as a genius. He was not only beating his mates in academics but also giving some of his teachers anxious moments by some of his out of the blues intelligent questions, especially teachers that did not prepare for their lessons. One of his teachers, Mr Binda Kiama, could not hide his preference for him. If for any reason he was not in school on a particular day, Mr. Binda taught his class with an attitude that showed he felt something important was missing in the class. This made Ahoka unpopular with some of his fellow students and they shunned his company. But because he was not too much of a social person, he cared little.

One day, during break-time, Mr Binda Kiama called him and asked him which primary school he graduated from before coming to Semina Secondary School.

'Ronfo Primary School sir,' said Ahoka who already could speak fairly flawless English.

'Are you telling me the truth?' Mr Binda asked, looking incredulous.

'Yes, sir,' he said.

For a good moment, Mr Binda said nothing. Ronfo Primary School was known in Beku as the most dilapidated and ramshackle primary school in terms of physical structures, and the most ill-equipped in terms of stationery and teaching staff. Its decaying ceilings and collapsing buildings told a sordid story of many years of neglect by the appropriate authorities: the Beku North local government and the Beku state government. Half of the school children took their lessons outside under the shades of trees without blackboards or textbooks. It was a lexicographer's perfect epitome of a black-eye. Even with the high level of unemployment in the Republic, not many teachers would accept a teaching appointment in the school. Only children of the poor attended the school.

'Why didn't you go to a better school?' Mr Binda asked at last.

'My father didn't have the money to send me to one sir,' he said at the brink of tears.

'Don't cry Ahoka my dear,' Mr Binda said, getting up from the chair he sat on by the classroom veranda to rock him in his arms. 'It doesn't matter which primary school you attended since you are streets ahead of the children that attended the best primary schools in town. Don't cry Ahoka my dear,' he said, releasing him from his arms.

He wiped away the tears that had already fallen on his cheeks and ran to the field to join other students in their morning physical exercise.

In his physical exercise group was a pretty-looking girl who kept looking at him. She was very light complexioned and had big bulging eyes. From her robust cheeks, it was obvious she was the daughter of rich parents. He wondered what she was doing in Semina Secondary School built only for children of the poor. Any time he caught her looking at him, she would quickly look away. When break time was over and they were going back to their classes, he was surprised to see her walking towards his classroom.

'Hi sister!' he said, increasing his pace to catch up with her. 'Are you telling me we are in the same class?'

She turned and saw him then her face lit up in smiles. 'Of course, we are!' she said in a melodious tenor voice. 'How can you know who is in your class and who is not when you are always by yourself.'

'But I know Jenks, I know Siyo and some other members of our class,' he said, smiling back at her.

'How won't you know Jenks when he is your friend and a loud mouth,' she said, walking beside him.

'Anyway, that is by the way,' he said in a matter-of-fact way. 'Why were you looking at me while we were playing at the field?'

'Because I want you to be my friend,' she said with a slight tremor in her voice.

He was shocked by her direct and blunt reply. 'Why do you want me to be your friend?' he asked, breathlessly.

'Because I like you,' she said. This time, the tremor was gone.

'Why do you like me?'

'Because I just like you,'

'But that is no answer.'

She said nothing

'What's your name?'

'Sindra.'

'Sindra who?'

'Sindra Lafimo.'

'Are you the daughter of the Great Lafimo?'

'Yes, I am.'

For some seconds, he did not say anything. He had heard strange stories about the Great Lafimo who was believed to be the richest man on the whole of the West African coast. He dealt principally in ships; though he was also said to be a cocaine baron. Still some people said he printed and minted money, while others that he invoked it with the aid of supernatural powers. In fact, some years ago when a man was found electrocuted near an electric transformer, it was rumoured the man went to tap red mercury for him to render merchantable money so invoked. Whichever way he got his money the fact remained he was a very rich man. But he was also said to be a miserly fellow who would rather die by his money than part with any of it. In fact, it was once reported in one of the soft selling magazines that he was caught mending his own shoes. His miserliness probably explained why his daughter was in Semina Secondary School instead of one of the colleges of reputed academic excellence attended by children of the rich.

'Why are you silent?' she asked, interrupting his thoughts.

'Oh,' he said, raising his hands in a gesture that said, 'I am not thinking anything.'

'I have told you my name, but I won't ask your own name because I know you are Ahoka Solo,' said she, laughing.

'What can I say?' he said, laughing with her.

'But you have something to say,' she said. 'Tell me why you were crying this morning when our teacher Mr. Binda was talking to you.'

Just then the school's principal saw them standing outside their classroom and yelled at them to go in as break-time was over. Ahoka was grateful for the timely interruption and he was the first person to enter the classroom.

Since that day, he and Sindra became hot friends playing together during break-time and working out their assignments together. Sindra was always thrilled whenever Ahoka solved on the spot a seemingly difficult mathematics problem. She was generally weak at mathematics but good at Christian Religious Knowledge and spoken English. She had committed so many Bible verses to memory that Ahoka always addressed her jokingly as Sindra the prophetess. Whenever there was an assignment, they stayed back in school to solve it before going home. After school hours every day, Sindra's father's driver came to pick her home in their old Peugeot 504. Long before he arrived, Ahoka would have slipped away through a small path that linked the school with his home; unless they were given an assignment that day.

Ahoka had a male friend called Sozuwa but popularly known among his friends as Jenks. They were bosom friends and were often seen together in the school premises. Jenks was a gangling boy about Ahoka's age, lively and outgoing. Though he was Ahoka's friend, their character and intellect were seldom in concert of friendship. While Ahoka was something of a genius and unassuming, Jenks was a brainless, outgoing brag. He was all over the school boasting to fellow students that cared to listen that he was born in the United States of America and that he had arrived the Republic via an American airliner Boeing 707; and that as a matter of fact, his parents were still in the States and he would join them there after his secondary school education. This was the stuff he kept feeding Ahoka with to the point of driving him nuts. But since the day Ahoka and Sindra became friends, he completely went cold on Ahoka refusing to speak to him even when spoken to. Ahoka was worried. He could not see where he had offended his friend. One day during break-time, he asked him to escort him across the street to buy tom-tom sweet, but Jenks rudely rebuffed him asking him where a poor boy like him got the money to buy tom-tom. A fierce anger gripped Ahoka making him tremble. He gripped Jenks by the collar of his shirt and jerked him forward furiously. His grip was firm and choking.

Jenks let out a high pitch sound that a cat on fire would make.

'Talk again idiot and I will send your bowels back to the United States,' Ahoka rasped, breathing heavily. Jenks' eyes were out of their sockets and tears were rolling down his face. Breathing was becoming more difficult by the second.

'Ahoka what are you doing there?' he heard Mr. Binda Kiama's voice coming behind them. He immediately let go of Jenks and walked away.

From that day, he and Jenks became sworn enemies.

About a month after their open fight, Ahoka was not in school as a result of a splitting headache. Jenks looked round the classroom, but did not see him. He smiled to himself and waited impatiently for break-time.

During break-time, he walked confidently to Sindra standing forlornly behind their classroom and said, 'hello babe, do you care for some company?'

'No, I care for some factory,' she said, looking scornfully at him, then began to walk away.

He stood there looking at her then said, 'men, what do you know; this lass sure gets the knockers. Please babe don't run I ain't gona eat you. I only wantta tell you something; yeah, something pretty hot, babe.'

But she moved on not stopping. He ran after her and caught up with her by their classroom door 'Yeah, babe,' he rapped. 'Why run? No bull shit talk from me. You can be sure babe. You should be fussy who you talk to babe.'

Yep, that is why I don't talk to loons like you,' she said then burst into a derisive laughter when she saw a defeated and angry expression replacing the usual confident look Jenks wore around the school. But Jenks would not give up. He had started something. He must finish it. It did not matter if he had to finish it from a damned position.

'Not your stuff,' he ventured again. 'The yobbo sure stains your colourful parentage.'

'Who or what is not my stuff?' she asked, a mild look of bwilderment on her face.

'Ahoka,' Jenks replied rapidly.

'I thought Ahoka was your friend,' she said, moving from hostility to curiosity.

'That was what you thought and that was what the yobbo thought until he received his shocker. I ain't care a fig for the yobbo's stinking arse. But the yobbo sure gets some brain and I wantta to use his brain to pass, babe.'

'Tell me why you don't like Ahoka,' she said.

'Sure babe, sure,' he said, frantically, his face lightning up.'He is a son of the gutters living under some bridge between Desowa and Beku Island. Babe, does that kind of home give me the heebies?' he yakked on, shrinking his body.

Chapter Nine

The following day, Ahoka was in school and went straight to Sindra's desk. Her reception was cold and flat. He walked away to sit by himself at the right corner of the class surprised and despondent. What could have gone wrong during just one day absence from school? he wondered. At the left comer of the class, Jenks was beside himself with joy.

During break-time, Sindra walked to Ahoka and said, 'Ahoka I want to talk to you.'

Without saying anything, he followed her to a small eucalyptus tree standing at the edge of the school's football field.

'Ahoka, please tell me the truth, where do you live?' she asked in her usual down-to-earth manner when they came to rest by the eucalyptus tree.

The question hit Ahoka like a thunderbolt leaving him dumb. For a moment, everything stood still for him. Then his heart started beating wildly, his head spinning round and round turning Sindra into a flickering shadow before his eyes.

'Please, Ahoka, tell me the truth,' he heard Sindra pleading. He wanted to answer, to tell her the truth she was yearning for. But he could not; the fog in his head was becoming thicker and thicker. He stood there seeing her flickering before his eyes until she dissolved into nothing. He flopped down by the eucalyptus tree fighting to sail over the dizziness screaming madness in his head. After sometime, the dizzy feeling started ebbing carrying along with it the fog in his brain. He was beginning to see things clearly, but more importantly, to think. Sindra was no longer with him. 'Where has she gone to?" Not that he was so keen on her whereabouts as how she came about her knowledge of his residence. In his mind, only one person could have told her because only that person in Semina Secondary School knew his residence: Jenks his erstwhile friend.

Immediately after their open squabble, he realized his friendship with Sindra was the cause of Jenks' change from being a jovial friend to a bitter foe. Given his arrogant manners and boastful mouth, he would not be happy to see another boy in Semina Secondary School and not himself 'floating around,' to use his language, with Sindra who was by common consensus the most beautiful girl in Semina Secondary School. He was surprised he did not read his action in this light long before then. Jenks must have sweated bidding his time to strike at him with his only weapon, a smearing campaign, and to strike where it hurts most: Sindra his girl friend. The time came yesterday when he was not in school.

'Well,' he muttered quietly to himself. 'The truth she asked me, the truth I will tell her; what else can I do?' Tears came streaming down his cheeks. After sitting for sometime, he stood up to go back to the class; then he saw Sindra walking towards him with a bottle of coke. He stood looking at her as she walked towards him.

'Ahoka my friend.' she said as she drew near him. 'Don't go yet; sit down and take this bottle of coke; may be you will feel fine again.' There was a sad note in her voice.

For a split second, an angry bee with the claws of a bear clammed its fangs on his heart and a bitter voice, that disclaimed all allegiance to friendship screamed in the backwaters of his mind: 'Feel fine and tell you the truth distressful to me?' But his spirit of friendship promptly rebuked this voice and he took the bottle of coke from her. 'Thank you Sindra,' he said, an urge to cry taking root in him. 'You have been very kind to me; unfortunately, I am born of poor parents. What can I also do for you Sindra?' he said, shaking his head.

'Please, don't cry Ahoka,' she said, squatting down in front of him. 'I don't want you to give me anything; just tell me the truth.'

That is the truth,' he said in a shattered voice. 'My father and I live under one of the bridges between Beku Island and Desowa.'

For a long time, she stood looking at him saying nothing.

'Sindra, I know you will no longer want to be my friend, will you?' he asked, anxiously.

'Ahoka,' she said, blinking her eyes rapidly; 'thank you for telling me the truth. I am still your friend; it is not your making to be living under a bridge. It is because your father has no money.'

Then Ahoka's tears, which have been welling, broke out in torrents of grief. As he wept, his body shook. Sindra wept with him while trying to console him at the same time. After sometime, he was able to pull himself together. 'Thank you Sindra,' he said. 'I don't really know what is making you stick to me a boy from the sidewalks. But I know that you are not like other children of the rich who treat us a little lower than their basin sponges. You have a large heart. Thank you Sindra.'

'Forget everything Ahoka my friend,' she said. 'I will always be your friend. You are such a handsome, intelligent and truthful person. Worry not. We are even going to be hotter friends. Let the person who doesn't like our friendship continue to have bad dreams. Forever, we will be David and Jonathan.'

'It was Jenks who told you,' he asked, half statement, half question.

'Yes,' she replied. 'I was really horrified by the names he called you. I thought you were once friends?'

'Perhaps, we were,' he said, standing up. 'But we aren't now. Now we are worse than enemies.'

'What actually caused your falling apart?' she asked with a look of concern.

'You of course!' he said, giving her a mirthless smile.

'What do you mean me?'

'I mean Jenks never likes seeing me with you. He sees himself as the uncrowned prince of Semina with a birthright to all the good things of the school. You know you are one of those good things. So when he saw you and I becoming friends, he developed goose pimples and hatred for me.'

'I see,' she said, nodding her head. 'But, he must have bats flying in his head to think I will like to have a fool for a friend.'

'Oh, he is no refuse man,' he said, feigning indignation. 'He is only an ambitious American yankee.'

They laughed and walked back to the classroom as break-time was over.

Much to Jenks' chagrin and frustration, Ahoka and Sindra became more intimate friends after his *coup-de grace*. They were always walking and eating together during school hours. Sindra would have followed Ahoka home one day if her father's driver had given her the chance and if Ahoka himself had been forthcoming to let her know the bridge he called his home.

Whenever she said she would like to know which of the many bridges he was living under, he would say it is such a mean habitation undeserving of the presence of the daughter of the Great Lafimo. She pressed him day by day but he would not budge. Then tongues began to wag both in the school and outside. 'What is the daughter of the

Great Lafimo doing with a boy of the sidewalks? Why is she in Semina Secondary School in the first place?' The irony was that this tongue-wagging was among the poor. Whenever they saw the two youngsters walking together, they stopped whatever they were doing to stare at what they considered an aberration of normal human relations in the Republic. Even the Great Lafimo had gotten wind of the steaming friendship between his daughter and Ahoka. As fate would have it, the very day he learned of it was the day his daughter informed him of it and begged him to sign away one of his numerous houses in Beku or at least his boys' quarters to Ahoka and his father. The Great Lafimo went berserk with rage. He had waited patiently for his daughter to return from school to deny the woeful tale that had fallen into his ears only to hear her not only confirming it, but even suing for its explosion.

'I am warning you to steer clear of all sidewalkers,' he said when his anger had simmered down to a sane level. 'You have a million and one mates to choose as friends within our divide, why go to the gutter stock? What have you to gain from such a scrounging society?'

'But, daddy, you have always told us that you were born of poor parents living on the charity of men of goodwill.'

'And so what!' he stormed at her. 'That explains why you should run at the sight of a sidewalker. I never want to smell life in the gutter again. Too many spongers on our wealth will surely see us back in the gutters. See what I mean?'

She did not say anything; neither did she leave Ahoka. They only made sure they were not seen together as often as before especially by Lafimo's driver. But in their fourth year in Semina Secondary School, disaster struck. Ahoka was sent packing from school because his father could not pay the seven thousand rida demanded by the school authority pursuant to the newly introduced Book policy in all post primary institutions in the Republic. Under the policy, every parent was required to pay seven thousand rida to the school authority for each child he had in school. It did not matter at all which level of education the child was. The central consideration was that such a child was in a public school. According to the government, money realised from this levy would be used to purchase textbooks for the general students' use. But no student would leave the school with any of these books purchased with his money. 'This is aid to free education at all levels,' the Minister for Education had said. Ahoka's father together with other poor men with children in Semina Secondary School who could not pull out this amount in one dip of the hand into the pocket, went to plead with the school's principal for installments payment. But the principal would have none of that. He had directives from above that any student that did not pay the whole money after two weeks of the announcement of the policy by the minister must leave the school. So, when Ahoka's father together with other poor parents could not beat the deadline, their children were sent packing by the dutiful principal. Ahoka wept that day until his eyes were swollen. What had he done? Has poverty become a crime in the Republic? And even if it were, did he commit it? His mother died because they were poor. They were living under a bridge because they were poor; he was leaving school because they were poor. What pained him most was the jeering look of Jenks his erstwhile friend. He had sniggered at him when the principal called him and other students to share his fate to the front of the assembly to tell him why they had not paid their money for the Book policy.

'I have been informed by your teachers that you are a very brilliant boy,' the principal said, specifically addressing Ahoka. 'Why can't your father pay for your books?'

'He has no money sir,' he said, his eyes to the ground in fear and shame.

'What do you mean he has no money? How does he feed you?' the principal asked, heatedly.

'That is all his money can do sir,' he murmured, tears already on his cheeks.

'Sorry boy,' the principal said. 'There is nothing I can do. I am afraid, you have to leave the school until your father is able to pay this money. I am yet to see why other students should buy books for your bright head to consume. And 1 am warning you never to venture near this school until the money is paid. What I am telling him applies to all of you,' he said, addressing the other students called out to the front of the assembly with Ahoka. 'Now, you can all go home,' he said, dismissing them with the wave of his hand.

When Ahoka passed by Sindra, he saw her crying and covering her face with her school bag. Further down the same line, he passed by Jenks who giggled at him whispering, 'brilliant arse; so you gona leave school? Why ain't you taking your wench along, or she ain't your tail anymore?' He walked on crying and clutching at his notebooks that kept slipping from his damp hands.

For two weeks, he lay under the bridge weeping out the venom of his bitterness and frustration. His father pleaded with him to calm down to no avail. Nothing short of going back to school would console him. At the end of two weeks, he was dried of tears and seized by a strong determination to work, get some money and go back to school. But what work was there for him to do? he kept asking himself. It was clear he could not get a job in any of the factories polluting the air in Beku with their smoke and stuffing the gutters with their bloated waste. He knew that even university degree holders were roaming the streets looking for jobs that existed only for applicants enjoying ties with people in government or big-time business. In this set up, where was his place as a secondary school throwout and a child of a security man? Stealing, his body shrank from the very thought. With his own eyes he had watched armed robbers being shot at Pento firing squad. That apart, his father had always told him they came from a proud family of native doctors somewhere in Lamto city which forbade stealing and lying. If any of them should steal or lie, according to his father, whatever herb they gave would have no efficacy. He resolved not to steal. So how would he come by money in a land where even those *who* had it locked it up only to be heard rending the air with lamentations of how poor they were because of honest and patriotic service to their fatherland? Then he remembered having seen some children picking empty bottles from dustbin cans for sale to bottling companies in Beku. The following morning after his father had returned from his night duty, he took an empty fertilizer sack and stole away to Beku Island to join other children of his age scavenging for empty bottles, plastic cans and iron bars in the rubrics of dustbins.

For two years, he has been beating the streets of Beku Island, Voro and Desowa foraging for empty bottles and iron bars but he had not gotten enough money to see him back to school. Whenever he saved money that when combined with whatever contribution his father might make to him would see him back to school, the money got guzzled up by the galloping and endemic high cost of living in the Republic.

Chapter Ten

One rainy Saturday morning, Ahoka's father returned home to tell him he was on double duty as Berijo the other watchman had fallen sick. So Ahoka should stay at home to keep an eye on their belongings as he would be returning to office immediately. Though Ojoro could be trusted to watch over their property, he had as usual left the bridge for his unknown abode during the day.

Ahoka did not like this. Not that he enjoyed walking the streets picking old bottles. But that at least was less dreary than sitting chained to the bridge. Often, while walking the streets, he ran into other boys also rummaging for empty bottles. They got talking about their hopes and aspirations for the future. After such discussions, he would go home happy and relieved of his sorrows, even if for a while. On a lucky day, they might even stumble on a stale loaf of bread in a dustbin in Beku Island or Voro. Though, they often fought over any loaf of bread so retrieved, at the end, each of them would have a bite. But since his father had asked him to stay at home, he had to. He lay down and dozed off. When he woke up, the rain had stopped and the sun was shining brightly. For something to do, he stood up and walked to the lagoon. As he came to the shore of the lagoon, he saw a white man and a black man yachting on a skiff. He stood looking at them fascinated. Although yachting on the lagoon was almost an

70

everyday spectacle, especially on weekends, he never seemed to get tired of watching it.

Standing on the edge of the lagoon watching the two men yacht in turns, he observed that whenever it was the turn of the black man, the small board seemed to fly over the water and was never steady. Again, he never stayed long on the board before being thrown off into the water. He also noticed that a wolfish grin always lit his sagging face whenever it was his turn to manage the small board. He wondered what he could be grinning at. On the other hand, when it was the turn of the white man, the board maintained a steady and smooth sail. When he was tired, he would stretch one of-his legs and nudge the black man on his back who would immediately jump up with his wolfish grin on to take control. As the minutes ticked away, the wolfish smiles on the face of the black man began to irritate him, especially as he could not see what he was smiling at. He hissed and walked back to the bridge. He had hardly sat down when he heard a movement behind him. He spun round to see an elderly man of about fifty years and a woman much younger than the man walking into the bridge. They were wet and looked like something the cat brought in. The woman carried a big carton on her head while the man held two polythene bags in both hands. He could see clothes inside the polythene bags.

Without saying anything to him, the two strangers walked past him and put down their bags and baggages on the same side of the bridge, a little to the west of where he was standing. He became very angry. Over the years, he had come to regard this part of the bridge as their home and property. Nobody had yet challenged the propriety of his claims on the bridge so far. From where did these rude trespassers spring from then? How could they just walk into their house without even the courtesy of greeting him? He was sure they were mad people. He walked to them and asked, where una from come our house, wey una no fit talk to me, but come sit down as if una dey for inside una yard?'

'So na una build dis bridge?' the man asked, looking at his wife who was trying to remove something from one of the polythene bags.

'No be we,' he said, seething with anger. 'But, na we first come live for here.'

'Make una come hear me yeye talk,' the man said, breaking into a loud laughter.'So because una first come, naim come make the bridge una own?' he asked.

'So my talk don become yeye for una ears, ehn?' he asked, now angered more by the man's unperturbed behaviour than even his supposed violation of their privacy. 'Fine, by the time my papa come back, we go know who dey talk yeye talk,' he went on, biting his lips. 'Even sef, I no go fit wait foram; na him office I dey go so to bringam come see snake wey wan comot rabbit for him hole.'

'You never begin say anything yet,' the man said, a faint smile playing on his lips. 'You for say you go call President because naim get bridge. But dis one wey you dey talk about your papa, na jankara talk be dat.'

He did not say anything as he ran to Beku Island to tell his father about the unruly strangers in their home. When he got to the Okimes' he was sweating and breathless. He shook the gate and waited, but nobody peeped out from the small cabin at the gate to know who was around.

Silently, he opened the small gate and peeped into the small cabin but his father was not there.'Where could he have gone to?' he wondered. As he stood by the cabin wondering what to do, a corpulent and walloping looking woman opened the front door of the main house and stomped towards him. It was Mrs Okime.

'What do you want here?' she howled at him from a distance.

'I came to see my father,' he said.

'Who is your father here?' she asked, coming close to him.

'Your watchman ma,' he said.

'If your father is our watchman does that entitle you to come gatecrashing into our house any time it thrills your fancy?'

'Sorry ma,' he said, avoiding her hostile face. 'But I don't always come here. Even today, I came because there is something important I want to tell him. True ma.'

'Can the child of a wretch ever be relied on for the truth?' she said with unnecessary violence. 'If he tells the truth, who will take after his lying and thieving father?' She turned and walked back to the house. When she got to the terrace, she wheeled round and motioned at him to come.

Feeling miserable, he sauntered languidly towards her. When he reached her, she opened the door and walked in. He followed her. She took a cursory look at him then hissed, 'your father is down there,' she said, pointing in the direction of the kitchen.

If the outside of the house was beautiful, its inside was downright splendid. Everything looked and smelt money. The walls were of glasses reflecting you wherever you turned. There were about three different types of rugs spread on top of each other. The curtains were sea blue dotted with white spots. The blinds were pure white. From the ceiling hung rope-like electric bulbs going on and off intermittently. Further down the room was a giant size coloured television showing a wrestling contest. He felt dizzy and punch drunk in the middle of all these.'How does one pick his way in this maze of beauty?' he wondered.

'Didn't you hear me?' Mrs Okime barked at him with unrestrained anger. 'I thought, I said your father is working in the kitchen down there?' she said, pointing in the direction of the kitchen again.

He followed the direction of her hand and found his father washing plates inside a sink in the kitchen. 'Papa you no be watchman again?' he whispered so as not to be overheard in the sitting-room.

His father turned and saw him. 'Ah, Ahoka my pikin, na you?' he asked, his erstwhile cloudy face brightening up. 'Make you no talkam my pikin. Na me be watchman and na me come be cook. And all dis for six thousand rida. You ever hear dat kind thing before? True, their wahala don dey tire me.'

'Papa,' he said, embracing his father. Tears were coursing down his cheeks.

'No cry my pikin,' his father said, holding him. 'We never die yet. One day, God go take good eye see us.'

He calmed down and sat on a tall stool in the kitchen.

'Wetin bring you come dis house today?' his father asked. 'I hope nothing happen for house?'

'Papa, wahala dey house o,' he said, standing up to pace round the kitchen.

'Wetin happen?' his father asked, dropping in the sink the plate he had just picked up to wash.

'Papa, as I dey wan lie down for house,' he began talking fast; 'naim I come hear noise for my back. I come look back and see one old man with him wife dey walka into our house. The wife carry one big carton for head and the man hold leather bags for hand. I come ask the man wetin bring them come our domot. E come tell me say no be we get the bridge; dat the bridge na gofmen property and dat na only President go fit drive dem comot the bridge. Naim I come run here to tell you the kind shakara wey don dey nack for our domot.'

'How the man be?' his father asked, sighing.

'Na tall thin man with biabia for face.'

'Wetin I go do now?' his father said under his breath.

'I know say madam no go gree me go home now wey no servant dey the house. Wetin I go do?' There was a long interval of silence before he said, 'the thing wey I see for dis kind shakara be say, you go go wait for me for house until 7 o,clock for evening. Then I go rush come see who born baboon pikin wey wan cause katakata for me.'

'Papa, me I no go go home alone o,' he said, shaking his head. 'I no wan see dat jibigti man alone? I go wait for you make we go home together.'

'But madam no go allow you sit down for kitchen here with me,' his father said in a pleading voice.

'Then I go sit down for the small room for gate wait,' he said quickly. 'Shebi, she no go say make I no sit down for yonder?'

'No, you fit go sit down there,' his father said in a sad tone. 'I go soon finish washing the plates sef. Then I go come join you for yonder.'

He walked out of the kitchen and out of the house to the small cabin at the gate. There was a long wooden plank lying on three blocks of cement inside the cabin which served as a bed and chair

for the watchmen. He lay down on it to wait for his
father.

Chapter Eleven

Ahoka was searching for a box of matches to light their rickety stove when he came by the ragbag he picked off a dustbin along Landscape Avenue a couple of weeks ago. He had almost completely forgotten about it. Like he picked it from the dustbin, he picked it and tucked it into a trousers pocket and went on with his search. He searched everywhere but he could not see the box of matches. His eyes wandered across the bridge to where Bewudi the trespasser sat facing him eating a roasted yam. When their eyes met, Bewudi wheeled round on his buttocks to face the other side, his teeth munching the yam.

A wave of anger shot through him as he stood staring at Bewudi's back. It was three weeks since he came to live under the bridge with them. When he and his father arrived the bridge from Beku Island the rainy Saturday Bewudi and his wife came, they met only the wife under the bridge.

'Where your husband go?' his father asked, standing with his hands akimbo.

'Me, I no know o,' she said. 'E just comot walka go dat side,' she added, pointing to the bush.

'Which kind husband e be?' his father asked surprise and anger on his face. 'How person go come dump him wife for place e no *know* comot leaveam for yonder. Shebi him head dey correct?'

'I sure say my head dey correct pass una own,' Bewudi said, coming behind them.

'Baboon pikin!' his father cried, wheeling round. 'You think say you don land, na lie! Na you I dey wait for. I go show you say you never land. You still dey for air,' he went on snapping his fingers at Bewudi.

Bewudi did not even look at him. He walked past them with a dignified gait, his shoulders hunched up.

'OK chicken yansh,' his father said, giving Bewudi a chopping blow at the back of his neck with the edge of his palm. 'Here is your shit for hand.'

Bewudi lurched forward and fell on his face, his teeth digging into the loose lagoon soil. His wife covered the distance between her and him sprawled on the ground in three flying strides and collapsed on top of him crying. He and his father walked away to their own part of the bridge without saying anything. The following day Bewudi came to tell his father that whether he liked it or not, he was going to remain on that side of the bridge with them. According to him, he could not see how they were better entitled to the bridge than he and his wife. His father did not say anything.

During the night, he had considered the matter in his mind and came to the conclusion that he would not force Bewudi to leave his side of the bridge if he did not want to. After all, he did not build the bridge as Bewudi had pointed out. Come to think of it, Bewudi's presence might serve useful purposes in some respects. For instance, he felt he lacked human company. At his duty post, he spent all the time opening and closing the gate for cars to drive in and out. No one to talk to. At home, he came into the bridge through one side while Ahoka and Ojoro went out through the other. If he wanted to talk to anyone, he had to walk to the other side of the bridge. With Bewudi now on the same side of the bridge with him, they would be passing their days talking away their troubles. Also, now that his job appeared to know neither day nor night, Bewudi's presence would be of immense advantage as Ahoka could safely go out to hunt for bottles since Bewudi or his wife would keep an eye on their property.

But contrary to all expectations, Bewudi proved to be the serpent in their garden. He passed his days doing nothing and speaking to no one, even to his wife. When he was spoken to, he barked out like a dog that was being driven from a bone thrown before it. Worse, they began missing their things one after the other. If it was not a box of matches, it would be their money; if it was not their money, it would be their spoon. But, Bewudi always swore he had no hand in the missing things. As a matter of fact, he claimed to be missing his property also. It was as if some invisible spirit had come to live under the bridge with them whisking away their property under their very eyes. Every time he complained to his father, he would tell him not to worry as everyday is for the thief but one day for the owner of the property.

'Dis your talk, me I no likeam papa,' he protested one day when they could not find their ten rida note and his father in his stoical manner shrugged his shoulders and told him not to worry for surely all days cannot be for the thief.

'Everyday na so you dey tell me not to wori as one day God go deliver the thief for our hands; why dat one day never come, ehn papa?'

'Make you no wori my pikin,' his father said, patting him on his back. 'One day, dat day go come and e come for time wey you and the thief no dey expectam. True my pikin.'

So they went on living like cats and rats without any shade of trust. At a point, he and his father even thought of moving to another bridge, but it seemed all the bridges in Beku had been taken up by other homeless destitute so they had to stay put.

Standing in their own part of the bridge staring at Bewudi's back, he felt like strangling him. He walked softly across the bridge to where he sat and kicked him hard on the back.

Bewudi gave a siren-like yell as his head shot forward to hit the ground before him. The yam he was eating, flew out of his hand to land on the grass some metres away. He stood looking at him, his fists clenched. They were the only two people on their own side of the bridge that day. His father was on one of his double duties, Ojoro as always was away and Bewudi's wife had gone to the market to hawk some tomatoes he brought the previous evening. Bewudi gradually rose to a kneeling position and moved round on his hands and knees to face him. Foam was coming out from the left side of his mouth.

He stood watching every move he was making. Suddenly, Bewudi shot out his right hand to grab one of his legs, but he saw the move and jumped clear. The force of his thrust jerked him forward to fall on his face again. His mouth hit the ground and he cried out like a suffocating pig.

'Today na today,' he said sweat all over his body. 'You must give me our box of matches wey you don tif. Everyday my papa dey talk say every day na for the thief, but one day na for the owner of the property. Me I no go wait for dat one day again. Everyday go be for me and no day go be for you again. I hope you dey hear me well, yeye old man,' he went on, breathing down on Bewudi who remained sprawled on the ground refusing to sit or stand up.

He took a handful of dust and poured it on his head; then picked his empty fertilizer sack and moved towards Desowa. Moving through the crowd in Desowa market to Sefawa dunes where he usually searched for empty bottles, he felt somebody nudging him on his right shoulder. At first, he thought it was the usual rubbing and scratching of a crowded market. So he moved on without looking back. But the nudging persisted in a definite pattern forcing him to look back.

A boy about his age was on his heels smiling at him. He also had an empty fertilizer sack slung on his shoulder. He did not say anything, but walked on until they were out of the crowd.

'Why you dey touch me?' he asked, turning round to face the boy once they were out of the market crowd.

'Because 1 wan make we walka together,' the boy said still smiling at him.

'You know where I dey go?' he asked.

'I know now,' the boy said with an air of confidence. 'No be to find bottles?'

He allowed his question to ride then asked, 'why you wan walka with me?'

'Because I like you,' the boy said.

Suddenly, he felt like crying. These were the exact words Sindra used when he asked her why she wanted to be his friend. Why were people liking him and the world hating him? He turned and walked on without saying anything.

'But why you no tell me dat you like me also, or you no like me?' the boy asked, moving very close to him.

'I like you,' he murmured in a tearful voice.

'My friend, you wan cry?' the boy asked overtaking him to plant himself in front. Tears were already on Ahoka's cheeks.

'Please, my friend, don't cry,' the boy pleaded, looking very sorrowful. 'My friend, don't you like me, please don't cry.'

He wiped away his tears and patted the boy on his shoulder and moved on.

'I know say you be good person,' the boy said, falling into steps behind him. The smile was back on his face.

'Wetin be your name my friend; my own na Kela.'

'I be Ahoka,' he said, praying the boy would leave him alone for a moment.

'Ahoka, your name na fine name. Even sef, na dat name wey my brother wey dey Zodo for north dey bear.'

He did not say anything.

'Ahoka, na for where you dey live?' Kela asked

'Shebi, you no go leave me alone?' he shouted at Kela without looking back.

'Sori my friend, I mean Ahoka,' Kela said with innocent humility; 'I no mean to vex you. Please make you forgive me.'

'OK, no problem,' he said. feeling sorry for Kela.

'I hope we still be friends?' Kela asked, hopefully.

'Yes, we still be friends Kela,' he said.

By this time, they were already in Sefawa dunes and they went their separate ways in search of their wares. But, before they parted, Kela said, 'my friend, shebi we go meet here and walka go home together?'

He nodded and moved to the left; Kela moved to the right. Kela was the first to return to their point of separation. He put his sack of bottles down and waited for Ahoka. He soon joined him and the two started walking back home together. They had not walked fifty metres when Kela said, 'shebi, you hear wetin dem talk for television yesterday night?'

Wetin dem talk?' he asked in a tired voice.

'Mmm... my friend,' Kela said, bubbling with excitement. 'The thing wey dem talk na sweet thing o.'

'Wetin dem talk?' he asked, fast losing patience with his garrulous friend.

'The thing wey dem talk na sweet thing well, well,' Kela repeated not disturbed by the note of impatience in Ahoka's voice. 'Dem come talk say one madam wey her name be Mrs Narosi wey dey live for Voro dey look for the ring wey her husband wey don die take marryam. Dem say the ring lost about two months ago and the madam no sabi where she take losam.'

'Wetin dey sweet for dis kind tori?' he asked with a measure of anger when Kela seemed to have come to the end of his tale.

'The sweet part for the tori never land yet,' Kela said, letting out a guffaw. 'Naim I dey prepare how I go disham to you my friend,' he went on happy with the suspense he imagined he was creating. 'Dem come talk say anybody wey find the ring takeam to the rich madam, she go giveam se-ven hun-dred thou-sand ri-da,' he said, letting the words rolled out from his lips in spots.

'Wow!' Ahoka cried. 'You sure say dis tori na true?' he asked Kela, excitedly.

'Of course, na true,' Kela said. 'Na for my korokoro eyes and big, big ears dem nackam for television.'

'Where man pikin go jam dis ring for road?' Ahoka said, half to himself.

'Naim be say no more bottles foram be dat,' Kela said in his usual rustic manner.

'But come o,' Ahoka said, his voice rising, 'where dis madam come jam plenty money like dat?'

'Wetin you dey talk?' Kela asked. 'Shebi, I never tell you say her husband wey don die na General for army?'

'You never tell me o.'

'Then I dey tell you now.'

'Na wa o.'

'You now see wetin dey sweet for the tori?' Kela asked, beaming at Ahoka. 'But the thing wey bitter for inside be say no be one of us go finam.'

'You don talkam finish.'

They walked the remaining way in silence each buried in his hope and despair. When they got to Desowa proper, Kela said he would leave Ahoka there as he lived in Desowa. They shook hands and parted. Ahoka finished his way home thinking of the lost ring and the seven hundred thousand rida reward.

Chapter Twelve

7, 8, 9, 10.30 am, Ahoka was yet to see his father back from work. It was a Sunday morning, the only day they spent together under the bridge. He wondered what could be holding him back in Beku Island. If it were a week day, he would have thought he was on one of his frequent double duties. But it was Sunday, the day Okime never asked him to stay on double duty. Even on days he went on double duty, he always informed him beforehand. When it struck 10.30 by their old metallic clock that stood on a small flat wood, he put on his shirt and started walking to Beku Island. He could no longer contain the fear that kept making his heart lurch. By Seconde Street in Beku Island, a fast moving police van driven by men from the Flying Squad sped past him blaring a high pitch siren. There was a screeching and squealing of tyres as the driver of the van sharply applied his foot on the brake to negotiate the turn where Seconde Street melted into Fariche Street. The van jumped and skidded off the road, but the driver managed to bring it back onto the roadway even as he sped on. When the van got to Okime's house on Fariche street, again there was a screeching and squealing of tyres as it came to a storming halt by the gate. Four uniformed policemen jumped out of the van and flung open the gate with the violence and arrogance of policemen on duty. They were all armed with long rusty rifles.

When he saw the van stopping by Okime's house, he broke into a tearing race towards the house, his heart in his mouth. 'What could have happened to bring policemen to the house in this large number and at this neck-breaking speed?'

When the policemen got to the front door of the house, their leader a fat, belligerent police inspector who went by the name Onisuru rapped his knuckles on the door, 'hey bogeymen!" he bellowed. 'The fuzz are around, open up!'

A chilling silence greeted them. 'Hobos, I say open up and come out clean, the blues are around!' Inspector Onisuru who prided himself as the most eloquent speaker of English language in the whole of Beku police force yelled bombastically.

Again, there was silence. Somewhere inside the house a grandfather's clock began to chime 11.00 a.m.

Inspector Onisuru stepped back and gave the door a violent kick. The door flew open small splinters of wood falling on the terrace. He and his men walked into the sitting room with their guns in firing positions.

Ahoka stood by the gate wondering what had happened and what the police were doing inside the house. He wanted to enter the house, but bloodcurdling tales he had heard of police brutality would not let him. After what seemed like an eternity, Onisuru and one other policeman came out of the house. They were out so abruptly that he had no time to duck out of sight even if he had wanted to.

'Bee shed off your wings!' Onisuru cried when he saw him. Together with the other policeman they ran towards him by the gate, their guns at the ready. He stood where he was his mouth hanging open in fear.

'Your hands in the air,' Onisuru shouted at him as they drew near the gate.

He raised his hands up. Onisuru began frisking him from head to toe but found nothing.

'Where is your gun?' he asked, jerking one of his ears.

'Which gun?' he groaned in pain.

'Fine!' Onisuru said, thick saliva flying from his mouth. 'You will tell me which gun by the time you passed through the grill. I have handled tougher bees than you before and boy did they talk? Just wait till we get to headquarters,' he said, bundling him into the front seat of the police van. 'Corporal Sanda!' he cried, jumping into the front seat with Ahoka. 'Police headquarters under a beat!'

The policeman with him jumped into the driver's seat and the van took off with a cloud of dust. It was a Sunday morning and Beku streets were free of the usual traffic hold ups. Ahoka sat huddled up between the huge frame of Inspector Onisuru and Corporal Sanda his mind in turmoil. 'What on earth is all these about?' He had come to see what was keeping his father in Okime's house; he had not seen him and now he was being driven to police headquarters because he had not produced a gun he did not have.

'Sir, but this bee doesn't strike me like the stinging type or what do you think?' he heard the corporal saying.

'You can never tell,' Onisuru said curtly.

'But you can always have an idea,' the corporal said, 'at least from the face of the bee.'

'Are you paid to catch criminals or to have ideas?' Onisuru snapped.

'My tongue in my cheeks,' Corporal Sanda said, engaging gears. They drove the remaining way in silence.

As the van gradually ground to a halt before police headquarters gate in Joko town, Inspector Onisuru jumped down holding Ahoka by his shirt. The force of his fall jerked him out of the van to sprawl on the ground.

'Yeah, bee,' he said, shoving him through the gate.

'Here you go into the muffler. When you come out, you will come out clean.'

Ahoka's head hit the irongate and he slid to the ground. 'Get up bee, get up!' Onisuru shouted, sweat running down his fat face. 'This is just the mouth of the muffler. By the time you are in, boy will you sweat?' He jerked him up and dragged him by his shirt to the office of chief superintendent of police Mr Jakore.

Mr Jakore was a short man with a pot-belly that was out of all proportion with his thin frame. One could not look at him without being reminded of a kwashiorkor victim. Everybody wondered how he got into the police force, which places high premium on height and fine physique. But Jakore more than made up in intelligence and administrative adroitness for what he lacked in physique. People who knew this aspect of him wondered why he had not been promoted to the rank of assistant commissioner of police.

Ahoka and Onisuru found him sitting on his table, his short legs intermittently beating against the side of the table. His balding head was gleaming against the sunrays coming through the back window of his office.

'Yeah, sir,' Onisuru said, barging into the office with the arrogant air of having accomplished a difficult task. 'Here is one of the bees that did the shooting in Okime's house. And what a shooting sir! There is no single mosquito flying in that house. Talk of a holocaust and the Okimes come to mind.'

Jakore squinted at Ahoka then said, 'all right Onisuru, all right. Let's go over it bit by bit and see' what we have on our hands.' He dropped from the table and walked round to sit on his chair. When he had settled down comfortably in the chair he said, 'OK Onisuru, let the snail shell go burst; I want the snail on my palms.'

'Yes, sir,' Onisuru said, enjoying every bit of what he imagined to be his greatest achievement since he joined the police force some five years ago. 'As I was saying,' he began licking his lips, 'we drove off from this place like bullets from a barrel and got to Fariche in a jiffy. We ran up the house, guns in hand, on the lookout for trouble. I rapped on the front door two times calling on any bee inside to fly out with its wings in the air, Onisuru, Inspector of Police and his men are on the terrace. No door opened and no bee flew out. So we smashed our way in. And what did we find? Okime sat on the floor against a cushion chair with a clean hole on his temple. Mind you sir, it is not his lower hole put up, but a bullet hole,' he said, laughing.

'Do you have to be vulgar?' Jakore snapped, his eyes blazing.

'Sorry sir,' he said without looking sorry. 'I was only trying to clarify matters.'

'Do you consider me such a numbskull as not to appreciate the difference?' Jakore asked, heatedly. 'At least if you can't credit me with average intelligence, you can't credit me with stupidity either.'

'Sorry sir,' he said, this time looking it. The anger burning in Jakore's eyes had warned him to tread softly. The last time he toyed with Jakore, he received a strong query from the state commissioner of police. From the tone of that query, he knew any word from Jakore casting him in bad light would give him the chop off out of the police force and he was not kidding himself he could find another Job.

'No problem,' Jakore said, relaxing his face. 'I was only trying to make you be serious. A man has been murdered and you are making a joke out of it; is that a fine way to behave?'

'No, sir.'

'OK, go on.'

'As I was saying,' he began, 'Okime sat on the floor with a bullet hole on his temple; his wife lay naked near their coffee table with blood all over her body especially her thighs. From the look of things, she was raped before being shot. Their children lay spread- eagled inside the toilet with their throats slit.'

Ahoka who sat listening was surprised that Onisuru did not mention his father among the corpses. Where could he have gone to when the slaughter was going on? What could have happened to him?

'What of their househelps?' Jakore asked, 'or don't they have any?'

'Yeah,' Onisuru said putting on a look of being in deep thought. 'I can remember seeing a watchman there during one of our regular night patrol of the area.'

'Was he among the corpses?'

'No, sir.'

'So, what do you imagine could have happened to him?'

'That is the angle that has me foxed,' Onisuru said, looking vegetative. 'But he could have swung the job,' he suddenly blurted out excitedly. 'Damn me, why didn't I figure it out this way before?'

'Was anything missing?'

'Not as far as we could see.'

'So why should he kill them, for the fun of it?'

Onisuru did not say anything.

'Well, let's leave that angle for now,' Jakore said, fixing his eyes on Ahoka. 'What of the piece you bundled in here; where does he fit in?'

'Yeah, I was coming to him,' Onisuru said, brightening up. 'As we were coming out of the house to make a report to you of the mayhem that has been played out on Fariche Street, we saw this crab ducking behind the fence. 1 bolted after him and caught up with him even before he could decide whether to surrender or make a dive for it.'

'What did he say he was doing there?'

'What else sir, but taking potshots at the Okimes?' Onisuru said with a look of surprise on his face. Why should Jakore be asking such a stupid question he thought.

'Still, did you ask him?' he heard Jakore asking again.

'I felt there was no need.'

'What you felt and what you should have done are two different things.'

'Sure, sir.'

'So did you ask him.'

'No, sir,'

'But you should have done that? Prudence requires that when a bishop is found in the prison yard with inmates, he should not be rounded up together with the inmates to the prison farm. This chap strikes me as a bishop, not a murderer.'

'But, sir you never can tell,' Onisuru said in a faint, cracked voice.

'True, one never can tell, but one can see. He doesn't look a murderer to me.'

'As you please sir,' Onisuru said, his face falling to pieces.

'Yes, my boy what were you doing at Okime's house where my men picked you?' Jakore asked Ahoka.

'I went to see my father,' he answered, looking up at Jakore.

Onisuru hit him hard on the head with his baton. 'Who are you kidding?' he blared.' Seeing you, does anyone need a genealogy expert to tell him you are from the gutter stock? Who is your father on Fariche street?'

Ahoka gave a faint, tight scream, then stretched out on the floor.

'Come here,' Jakore said quietly to Onisuru. There was a wild expression on his face.

Onisuru did not move.

'Should I take it you are now the boss around here?' Jakore asked in a cold flat voice. The threat was unmistakable.

Onisuru took two steps and stopped near the table.

'Give me that baton,' Jakore commanded.

He handed the baton to him.

'Lie, down on the floor by him.'

Onisuru remained standing.

'I hate repeating my commands,' Jakore said, looking evil.

Onisuru lay face down.

Jakore brought down the baton hard on the back of his head. Onisuru rolled on his sides shrieking and kicking his legs.

'Get up idiot!' Jakore shouted at him. 'This is no Third-Degree Force; so you don't go wild on me. Before you tie a murder charge on our necks, I will see to it you are not only out of the force but out of your stinking yellow life as well.'

Onisuru stood up with his hands at the back of his head while his body hovered limply over the table.

Jakore went and touched Ahoka. He stirred at his touch and opened his eyes.

'Yes, my boy, sit up and tell me the story you were telling me,' he said, helping him to sit up.

'Who is your father in Okime's house?' he asked after Ahoka appeared to have recollected himself.

'He is one of their watchmen, sir.'

'Why did you go to see him?'

'Because he did not return from work since he left home yesterday sir.'

'What time does he normally close from work?'

'Six o'clock in the morning sir.'

'So since the Okimes were murdered early this morning, he must have been around when the massacre was going on. Onisuru, do you think he could have shot the Okimes?'

'Sir, does this beg any thinking? Of course, he murdered them!' he said, thick headedly.

Ahoka looked at him with all the hatred he could muster, then looked away.

Fine, you can look at me to your fancy,' he said, grinding his teeth. 'When next I handle you, you would be squeaking from your two holes.'

Jakore bit his lips.

Onisuru walked away from the table to stand by the door.

'Do you really think their watchman murdered them?' Jakore asked, his eyes probing Onisuru's face.

'Of course, sir,' he said. 'Hold him as the murderer and the jigsaw clicks; remove him and the whole thing falls to pieces with neither heads nor tails. He was supposed to be the watchman of the Okimes; the Okimes were found dead with bullets and knives hacking them to pieces. He is nowhere to be found. Tell me from this damn picture where is the way out for him? If he is not the murderer, we may as well be.'

'Yes, I guess you are right as far as your eyes can see or as far as your zeal would allow them see," Jakore said. 'But ask yourself this simple question, how could one man have murdered five people without any of them getting ideas of stopping him.

If they were all shot dead, one would have been tempted to go along with that line of thinking. But as it were, the three children of Okime were slaughtered one after the other under their very eyes. I mean this does not hang together with common sense.'

'This clinches it!' Onisum cried, cavorting on the doorway. There you got it! The yokel before you is an accomplice to his father. 'Who else would he hire to help him murder the Okimes when he has a yokel looking as mean as this?'

'Didn't Okime have other househelps?' Jakore asked, annoyed with himself for allowing Onisuru with his stupidity and bias turn of mind to dictate the type of questions he had asked so far, hence he had not come near to deciphering the kind of Jigsaw puzzle he was faced with, not to talk of fitting the different pieces together to form a persuasive picture with which to hunt for the murderers. 'Enough of the fooling around,' he told himself.

'Yeah, I have forgotten about that angle,' Onisuru said, scratching his head. 'Come to think of it, he had a cook and a gardener.'

'You better be sure,' Jakore said, looking grim.

'I am sure sir.'

'Did you know Mr. Okime personally?'

'Yes, sir.'

'Will you say he was the type that could so antagonize his servants to the extent that they would be happier with him dead than alive?'

'Yes, sir.'

'In what ways?'

'Well, he had this arrogant way of calling his servants snapping his fingers as if he were calling a dog, although all the sharks living in Beku do almost the same thing.'

'But they have different servants,' Jakore pointed out.

'What do you mean by that?' Onisuru asked, looking vacuous.

'Never mind,' Jakore said. 'I like this line,' he went on as if talking to himself. 'It makes the story a lot less taller. But there is a brainteaser in it and if care is not taken, it will bring the whole line crashing down on us like a pack of cards. It is not human experience that servants would wipe out their master and his entire household and then vanish into thin air without picking as much as a needle from the house.'

'I thought as much,' Onisuru chipped in for something to say.

'Let's get weaving to Fariche Street and nose around,' Jakore said, getting stiffly to his feet. 'It seems sticking around here talking all day is not getting us anywhere. I believe in playing it by the ear.'

'What happens to the crab here?' Onisuru asked, pointing atAhoka.

'He goes home of course,' Jakore said. 'If we want him later we can always pick him up.'

'He is your baby sir,' he said, eyeing Ahoka the way a cat would eye a rat inside a hole.

'On our Way,' Jakore said, crowding him out of the office. 'As for you,' he said, turning to Ahoka; 'we will drop you at home. If we have any need of you in future, you will be picked up; you get me?'

'Yes, sir,'Ahoka said, following him out of the office.

Chapter Thirteen

When they got to Lupendu Street which curved into Seconde Street, Ahoka said he would be dropping there.

'All right my boy,'Jakore said. 'Which house is your house here?'

'That house without paint over there,' he pointed at a groove-like house some hundred metres away from Lupendu Street.

'Fine, my boy, go and sleep well,' Jakore said, waving him away as they drove off. 'If we need you, we will come for you there.'

Ahoka sauntered towards the house until he was sure Jakore and his men were out of sight then he turned and started walking back to Lupendu street. Once on Lupendu Street, he went into a tearing hurry to get home where he hoped to find his father having not found him in Okime's house. As he drew near the turn that would bring him to Bakandi way, which ran over his residence, a white BMW car rolled past him missing him by a hair's breadth. He Jumped onto the pavement and nearly fell down. What a Black Sunday, he thought. The car gradually ground to a halt a few metres ahead of him. The rear windscreen and window glasses were heavily tinted so he could not see who was inside. When he drew, closer to the car, the glass of the offside front window rolled down with a faint rustle. Inside the car sat Sindra, beautiful and smiling.

If he had seen his father behind the wheels perhaps he wouldn't have been more shocked.

'Hello Ahoka,' she said, her smile turning into laughter. 'Surprised to see me?'

'Where did you spring from?' he asked, his heart throbbing wildly.

'That is not important,' she said, cheerfully. 'The important thing is I am here.'

'That is true,' he said, moving from surprise to embarrassment.

'Hop in and let's go out on the town,' she said, opening the front door for him. 'We have so much to talk about and so much to laugh over.'
Laugh? he thought; 'for me I only have so much to cry over. He hesitated for a moment then slid in beside her.

She pressed the winder button and the glass rolled up. She switched on the airconditioner and gradually swung the car back onto the free Lupendu Street.

'How did you so easily recognise me?' he asked, sinking deeper into his seat.

'What do you mean?' she asked, laughing, 'Remember we were David and Jonathan in Semina.'

He let out a timid laugher.

'What have you been doing with yourself since you left us?' she asked, keeping one eye on the road and the other on him.

'What can one do in a country that has no place for one?' he said, mournfully.

'Cheers Ahoka my friend,' she said with a benign look. 'I will strive to get you a job. Only that my old man is not disposed to charity, you would have been working tomorrow. But never worry. I will try on my own to get you a job, a good one for that matter. I know the strings to pull and the coins to slip in.' She was driving fast towards Memu.

'To get a job?' he thought, dreamingly.

'Why haven't you asked me about Jenks, your friend she asked, interrupting his thoughts. 'Come to think of it, you haven't asked me about myself either.'

'Jenks is a bad guy,' he said. 'You know our friendship was long lost before I left Semina. I care for him as much as he cares for me. As for you, I need not ask; seeing you and knowing whose daughter you are, I know you have been faring well.'

'It is said the monkey sweats in its own way, but because of its hair, the sweat goes unnoticed,' she said with a broad smile.

'The monkey then is better off than the pig who wears his sweat like a second skin for all to see,' he said, his mind crawling back to its sweet zone – getting a job. He was so engrossed with the thought that he didn't know when they drove past his residence. When he looked outside and saw Memu's tall buildings looming towards them, he said, 'oh you shouldn't have brought me this far. Since yesterday I haven't seen my father. I should have gone straight home.'

'Why haven't you seen him?' she asked, a keen expression on her face.

He wanted to tell her his father left for night duty, but never returned and the massacre in Fariche Street, but on a second thought, decided against that.

'I have not been home myself,' he lied. It pained him to lie; it pained him more to lie to Sindra.

'Where have you been?'

'At a friend's,' he lied again.

'What happened to your head?' she asked, noticing for the first time the bruise where Onisuru had hit him.

'I stumbled and fell on the road,' he lied glibly. Sweat was running down his face and there was a tight feeling in his chest. How many more times would he have to lie to Sindra? he fretted.

'But it looks like you have been hit,' she said, her eyes searching his face.

He said nothing.

'I will take you home later,' she said. 'Let's go to Santumi cafe first.'

'But I want to see my father,' he almost pleaded.

'What is the matter with the star of Semina today?' she asked with a frown. 'A beautiful girl wants to take you out for lunch and you are whining like a ram in the hands of butchers?'

He saw the frown on her face and said, 'as you please Sindra.'

Nobody spoke again until they were in Santumi cafe. It was a small round building shaded by well trimmed umbrella trees. It was in the heart of Beku near the city hall. A plate *of eba* which was the cheapest meal one could order there cost six hundred rida and a bottle of soft drink drew a hundred rida. Only the rich patronized it.

They found only a few people around the cafe. This was Sunday when not only the roads but restaurants were deserted by the boisterous Beku crowd. The chef, a sleek, haughty-looking fellow who saw himself as the *cordon bleu* of Beku came to stand by their table. He looked at Ahoka and seemed not to make much of what he saw.

'Yes, ma,' he said, addressing Sindra. 'Na the usual fried rice, plantain and chicken pepper soup?'

'You have my order,' she said, 'and make it fast.' Turning to Ahoka, she asked,'what will you take.'

'Your order is good for me,' he said.

'You heard him,' Sindra said to the chef.

'Yes, ma,' he said, walking away

'Do you know that I am now in Koka University reading law?' Sindra asked as they waited to be served.

'Not until now,' he said, his heart sinking. 'So Sindra is now in the university?' His feelings were not those of jealousy but of anger with whoever had saddled him with the cruel lot he had been labouring under. Sindra that relied almost wholly on him for solutions to her assignments was now in the university reading law while he was still scratching the streets for empty bottles and plastic cans.

'And Jenks your friend who was always talking about the United States of America suddenly stopped coming to school when we were about writing our final exams for reasons nobody knew. Just two weeks ago, I learned from my friend Tokwa that he had actually flown to the States but as a cocaine pusher.'

'I see,' he said, feeling nothing.

The chef brought one plate of the meal ordered and placed it before Sindra. It was a slap-up dish.

'Where's the other plate?' Sindra asked, looking up at the chef.

'I no know say na two I go bring ma,' he said not hiding his low opinion of Ahoka.

'How many are we?' she asked, her voice thick with anger. 'When will you people begin to cultivate good manners around here?' she went on picking the plate of food to place before Ahoka. 'I mean one is really disappointed. OK, we are two; go and bring another plate, and make it to order.'

He slouched away looking vile and humbled.

'Eat now,' Sindra implored Ahoka who sat staring at the food. 'Don't mind the lousy fellow. He has never been any good.'

'That I can see,' he said half-mindedly. He began tucking in the food. The second plate arrived with their bill: one thousand, nine hundred rida. Sindra brought out a handful of rida notes from her handbag and paid. 'Maltina,' she said, picking up her cutlery. 'This time two because we are two.'

When they finished eating, they drove away from the cafe towards Shrimkatu.

'Where are we going?' Ahoka asked.

'Won't you relax for a moment?' Sindra said, slightly angry. 'I mean you are no longer the Ahoka I knew in Semina. That Ahoka was warm and pleasant company; this Ahoka is cold and jumpy. Are you sure, you are happy to see me again?'

'Sindra,' he said, genuinely touched by her hurt feelings; 'it is not that I am not happy that we are together again but that I desperately want to see my father. Something terrible has happened.'

'What has happened?' she asked, alarmed. She trod down on the brake and brought the car to a halt on the sidewalks.

'Nothing that concerns you.

'But it concerns you?'

'Yes.'

'Then it concerns me.'

'Sindra, you are such a warm and kind hearted person,' he said in an emotion charged voice. 'Like Jesus, you reach out to the poor.'

'But I would have been poor myself if my parents were poor,' she said. 'We all do our best. But fortune and misfortune in the end decide who would be what. What is this terrible thing you said has happened?'

He told her what had happened in Okime's house and his fear for his father.

'God!' she exclaimed, drawing in a long breath. 'You should have told me all these; we wouldn't have afforded the luxury of this frolic.' She made a U-turn to take Geda Expressway, which would bring them to Bakandi way that ran over Ahoka's residence. Once on Geda Expressway, she engaged gears driving at 130 km per hour. When they got to Bakandi way, she slowed down to take it. Ahoka sat looking at her surprised she hadn't asked him for direction.

'Sindra, you know my place then?' he asked not hiding his surprise.

'Of course, I know it backwards,' she said in a matter-of-fact way. 'Don't tell me the heavily bearded man didn't tell you I called on Friday. I have been waiting to hear you mention it, but you haven't so far.'

'You mean Bewudi? He didn't tell me. How did you get to know where I live?'

'I asked around and looked around,' she said, a faint smile playing on her lips. 'I have always asked around to no use. But a week ago I had my lucky break when I started looking around. Inside one of the bridges between Beku Island and Desowa, I saw your small school bag and I recognised it. So after close of lectures on Friday, I looked in but neither you nor your father was in, but this bearded man. I asked him about you and he said you had gone picking bottles and that your father was in Beku Island. I would have dropped by this evening if I had not run into you.'

'Sindra,' he whispered bereft of words.

'Ahoka.'

The journey to his residence took only ten minutes. They parked the car on the sidewalk before getting to the bridge, then walked under. Two ragged women passing by stopped to take a second look at the young lady from Eldorado going under the bridge behind one of their own with an I-am-at-home gait that did not make allowance for avoiding being soiled by the bush that lined the small path to the inside of the bridge. The expression on their wizened faces bore testimony of the feelings of shock and disbelief that surged through them against the strange spectacle they were beholding.

Ahoka and Sindra met only Bewndi under the bridge. There was still no trace of Ahoka's father. Ahoka asked Bewudi if his father had returned home in his absence.

For the first time, Bewudi was friendly and even appeared somehow worried. He greeted Sindra knowingly and said, 'I no seeyam o. But I hear for radio say dem don kill him Ogar and him pikins but dem no know wetin happen to him watchman, cook and gardener. Even sef, dem talk say other armed robbers don kill another rich man with him pikins for north, but dem no know wetin happen to him cook, gardener and watchman dem.'

Ahoka and Sindra exchanged glances.

'You dey sure of dis announcement wey come from north?' Ahoka asked.

'I sure well, well,' Bewudi said. 'Even sef, if una wait small, they go talkam again,' he said, twiddling the knob of his small radio. He got the station he wanted but Banta music was in the air.

Sindra drew a small stool and sat down while Ahoka remained standing.

After about four minutes during which nobody spoke, the voice of an announcer broke through the Banta music to say it was 2 o'clock pm time for state news.

Ahoka and Sindra froze to attention. First on the news highlights was the massacre of two renowned families in the Republic by assassins suspected to be their own servants, though they could also be hired assassins. Then the newscaster went on to give details of the massacre and ended by saying that the President of the Republic has put the Republican police force on the biggest manhunt in the history of the Republic. They must within the shortest possible time track down and put behind bars the insurgents rebelling against the knitted society of the prosperous Republic, where they would await the pleasure of the President: execution by the crudest means that would relieve the indignant feelings of the rich at the extermination of some of them.

What will become of this Republic?' Sindra said, taking her face in her hands.

'Only the devil can tell,' Ahoka said, pacing up and down.

'What is the Republic turning to?' Sindra said again, standing up, 'If families get wiped out by their servants, who is safe?'

'But my father will never kill,'Ahoka said, moving to stand very close to her. 'Besides, they said it could be hired assassins which looks to me more probable.'

'You may be sure of your father; but what of the rest?

Only God can tell.'

'I am going out to look for my father until I find him, dead or alive,' Ahoka said in a firm voice. 'I am very sorry this has happened. But I am assuring you my lather has no hand in the massacre of his master and his family. He may be poor; but he is not a murderer. This, I am sure. Sindra, we parted last under mournful circumstances,' he went on taking hold of her hand. 'We are parting again under similar circumstances. When next we meet, I hope it will be under better circumstances.' He let go of her hand and stepped back, his eyes fixed on her face.

'I am a bit shaken by this news,' she said, her eyes to the ground. 'So I can't object to our parting now. When I get hold of myself, I will be back here to know how far.'

'That I can understand,' he said. 'But, please Sindra, tell me if you believed me when I said my father has no hand in these killings.'

'I believe you Ahoka,' she said, quietly.

'Thank you Sindra,' he said, taking hold of her hand once more. For a split second, he thought he saw something like a longing in her eyes, but it went out the way it came. They stood facing each other for about a minute, then he released her hand and ran out of the bridge.

'Ahoka, please wait for me,' she yelled, running after him. 'I will take you to wherever you are going to look for your father.'

A hawk swooping down on the nearby bush rebounded with a flurry against Sindra's piercing yells flapping its wings violently.

'No, Sindra!' he cried back. 'Go back home to your parents. I have brought enough trouble upon your head as it is. It's my duty to find my father.'

The hawk increased the flapping of its wings.

Chapter Fourteen

'You don hear say madam don increase the money she go give the person wey find her ring?' Kela asked Ahoka as they were bending down picking bottles and plastic cans along Buwani Street in Voro.

'I never hear o,' he said without interest. It was four days since his father went missing. There was no area of Beku he had not trod looking for him but all his trekking and prying had come to naught. Everyday, he left home 6 a.m. and returned 7 p.m. He had spent the little money he had on feeding in makeshift restaurants. Now he had to abandon the search for a while and work for some money with which to stay alive to continue the search. Yesterday when he returned to the bridge after another tiresome and fruitless day, Bewudi told him Sindra called in his absence, but that she would call back the following day. That following day was today. But he could not stay under the bridge waiting for her with his enzymes screaming murder. He had to go out and work for some money. If she comes in the afternoon or evening, fine, he would be in, but if earlier, too bad, he would still be out. From reports he heard from people, the police have even been more thorough and ardent in their search for his father and his co-househelps than himself. But, so far, none of them had been arrested. Worst, two other cases of the butchery of the rich and their families had been reported from the east. Like in Beku and the north, their servants went into thin air after the massacre. Rich men were fast moving from apprehension to sheer panic. Perhaps, what scared the living daylight out of them was that in all these cases of a systematic extermination of their class, the assassins left the houses of their victims without touching their property. The motive of the killing then was clearly not to rob. What was it then? Was it to wreck vengeance? To ventilate bitterness and anger? Or was it a class war? Although they wished the negation of these questions, they bitterly had to accept what they were faced with was their affirmation. Some of them had sent away their servants and were performing their domestic chores themselves while others had simply handed theirs over to the police as they possessed murderous instincts. Even those of them who could still afford the luxury of retaining theirs were merely tolerating them. In two separate broadcasts, the President of the Republic appeared on television looking pale and visibly shaken. He appealed for calm among the rich as his administration was doing everything possible to bring to book the bunch of sidewalkers threatening to slice off the cream of the Republic. But very few rich people saw any cheer in these broadcasts, especially that no single case of arrest had been reported.

'My friend, why you no dey listen to radio?' he heard Kela saying.

'I no dey interested,' he said.

'But you suppose to dey interested,' Kela said. 'You see, na for radio and television wey dem dey talk better thing like dis. One million rida no be something wey poor man pikin go talk say him get no interest for.'

'Na one million rida she dey offer now?' he asked, his eyes popping out.

'Yes, my friend,' Kela said, beaming at him. 'Just imagine getting dat kind money; naim be say no sweat go ever flow your body again lalai.'

'Na wa o.'

'Another interesting tori my friend,' Kela said after an interval of silence.

He paused in his work and listened wondering what next was coming from the gasbag.

''Gofmen don talk dis morning say dem go give five million rida to anybody wey fit catch any of dis people wey dey kill dis sharks or wey tell police where dem go go catcham.'

This was news to Ahoka and the shock on his face made Kela laugh.' You don dey see why man pikin must sit by him radio dey hear better tori?' he said, laughing out raucously.

'I don dey see o,' he said in a drawl. 'But, where dem get dis plenty money wey dem dey promise people like dis at a time gofmen dey cry no money for Republic?'

'Wetin dey wori you?' Kela asked. 'So you dey listen to dat wayo tori wey dem dey nack to fool poor man so e no go cry even as hunger wan killam. If money no dey, why President never lean? Why e never wear dirty clothe? Why e dey ride expensive car? Why e no dey chop eba like we? Why him face and dat of him wife dey shine for enjoyment? Na me and you money no dey for; but e dey yangfu yangfu for gofmen and shark dem. When big man die or e lose something wey e like well, na dat time you go see gofmen and big man dey fly money for poor man's face.'

'Na wa o,' he said, sorrowfully.

'You no dey happy my friend?' Kela asked, searching his face. 'Me I happy well, well as dem dey kill dis sharks wey boku for we obodo Republic. Dem no good at all, at all. Na poor man come be dog to dey lick the shit comot dem yansh; what heartless people!' For a long while he said nothing. His face showed he was thinking.

'Poor man dey smell shit for shark yansh for dis country,' Ahoka said, miserably.

'You dey talkam,' Kela said. 'How I go know where any of dis people wey dey kill dis sharks dey live? I go run go tell gofmen collect five million rida. I too wan be shark.'

'You no go smell dat money,' Ahoka said. 'You no know say dis gofmen and tortoise na first cousins? You no fit trust any of them. If you tell them where dis men dey, they no go give you one rida. You go even dey lucky if dem no kill you.'

'You dey say something there,' Kela said.

'You go tell them I tell you.'

'E no go come to dat my friend.'

'My sack don full,' Ahoka said, shaking the bottles inside his sack.

'Na so my own don beleful,' Kela said.

'Let's begin dey go home then,' Ahoka said.

They walked home silently neither talking to the other. When they got to their parting point, they shook hands as usual and parted. They had not walked a hundred metres when Kela turned and shouted at Ahoka, 'my friend, na for we poor men dis people wey dey kill sharks dey fight!'

'Na so!' Ahoka shouted back with feelings. They waved at each other again and walked on to their different destinations possessed by the same thought.

Ahoka got home to find Bewudi lying on his back while his small radio blared reggae music. He motioned to Ahoka to come. He dropped his sack and walked to him.

'Make you sit down hear wetin gofmen dey talk put for radio,' Bewudi said.

He sat down on a small stool near Bewudi. After about a minute or more of reggae music, the baritone voice of an announcer came on the air, 'The announcement once again: Though the government of the Republic is still wondering if hired assassins, a rebel group or the househelps of rich people are behind the massacre of the rich of the Republic, the balance of evidence with government seems to suggest that it is the househelps that are revolting against their masters. The government of the Republic is by this announcement therefore advising all rich people still retaining househelps to hand them over to the nearest police station in their own interest. Two more families of the rich were found massacred this morning in Beku with their househelps as usual vanishing into thin air. Police are doing their best to halt the wildcat madness of the servants against their masters. Once more, government views the whole situation with all the seriousness it requires. You are advised to cooperate with government to help you. Signed, President of the Republic.

'Wetin you think say dey happen for dis monkey-chop-monkey Republic?' Bewudi asked Ahoka.

'How man pikin go know?' Ahoka said. 'The only thing wey I fit swear for be say no be the servants wey dey kill dem ogar and dem pikins, because I no see sense for dat kind tori. How poor man go kill him ogar comot leave the house without taking even common needle? I mean dat kind tori never enter my head at all, at all.'

'Na so me dey seeyam o,' Bewudi said. 'But you know say gofmen sense dey different from we sense and I don dey fear for we poor people for dis kind announcement wey dem dey make every second for radio. How man pikin no go fear for anything wey dem mention police name for inside?' he went on speaking more to himself and his troubled mind than to Ahoka. 'They fit jam you for road begin dey drag you dey go dem station say na you be houseboy to shark so, so and so and therefore na you killam; wetin you go fit talk? And with money promise scatter everywhere, even person mama go fit sellam to police say na him be houseboy to shark so, so and so. You know dis our obodo Republic don rotten finish.'

'No be fear the thing dey fear me, na vex e dey vex me,' Ahoka said at the end of his tethers. 'Last year wey cholera wan finish poor people for Fuada inside dis Beku, wetin gofmen do? And dis rida devaluation monster wey dey suck poor man like mosquito dey go, wetin gofmen dey do? But because some few sharks don wake up to find bullets and knives for breakfast naim person no fit get place to put him ears from gofmen announcement. Let anything wey wan happen, happen. My mama don die, my papa I no seeyam; na me go come talk say I no go die?' He got up and walked to their own side of the bridge and lay down. He wanted to sleep, but a naughty fly that kept flying into his nostrils would not let him. He stood up and walked to the lagoon to take a bath. He pulled off his shirt and trousers and threw them on the lagoon sand. The small ragbag he picked up on Landscape Avenue fell out of his trousers pocket. He bent and picked it up, then drew back the zip. A small golden ring fell from it onto the sand. He bent down and picked it up. He turned it round in his fingers, flames of excitement leaping from his face to dance on the ring. He let out a high pitch cry, quickly threw on his clothes and ran past Bewudi with the ring held firmly in his right hand.

Bewudi stood looking at him wondering if he had gone nuts.

Chapter Fifteen

Ahoka did not stop running until he got to the point he always parted with Kela. He stood there not knowing what to do. He had never bothered to ask Kela the location of his residence in Desowa. Now that he wanted him badly, he silently cursed the failing in his character that tended to make him stand aloof others. Desowa was an over-populated suburb of Beku with no streets or house numbers. Most of its houses were shacks and sleazy makeshifts. Even when you had been to a house before, it was not always easy locating it again on another visit. In fact, it was not uncommon for a new tenant in Desowa to mistake another house for his own.

He held out the ring and examined it carefully once more. 'God,' he muttered prayerfully. 'May this ring be Madam Narosi's ring. And if it is, may you give her the grace to honour her promise; amen!" he cried loudly, dropping the ring into the ragbag and zipping it up. He tucked the bag into his back pocket and stood wondering how to get Kela that afternoon. Then he remembered Kela once told him there were days he went picking bottles twice a day. He smiled to himself. But even if he was on double duty today, did he know which area he would go to for his second duty? It was an even chance that he might go to Voro, Beku Island or Sefawa dunes in Desowa. But, after much thought, he fancied him going to Sefawa dunes than either Voro or Beku Island. This was because apart from being near to his house, Kela, like he, feared and resented the rich's mean and beggarly reception of the poor in Voro or Beku Island. What was more, they had just returned from Voro, so he was not likely to go back there. That left Beku Island and Desowa. He picked Desowa. He started walking in the direction of Sefawa dunes. But he did not find Kela there. He started walking back feeling despondent.

'Hah my friend!' he heard the usually loud voice of Kela coming behind him.

He spun round to find Kela standing closely behind him, laughing.

'Where you from come?' he asked, also laughing.

'From dat big dune wey dey yonder,' Kela said, pointing at a big heap of refuse in a distance.

'How I no kuku see you?' Ahoka asked.

'I hide myself well, well,' Kela said, breaking into another round of laughter. 'My friend, shebi you too don dey operate double duty? I no blame you,' he went on without waiting for an answer. 'Republic don dey hard too much. To survive, monkey must not only sweat, e must bleed. But, my friend, where your sack?'

'No be double duty bring me come. Na you I come find,' he said with a wide grin.

'Why you find me come?' Kela asked, surprised. 'Shebi, you don join police and dem tell you say na me kill shark Okime, Demzua and other sharks dem?'

'Even if I be policeman, no be my friend I go catch sake of say e kill some rotten shark,' Ahoka said, the grin on his face becoming more expansive.

'I say you be good friend,' Kela said. 'Now, tell me wetin you come find me do?'

'Na about dat ring wey you dey talk about everyday,' Ahoka said, the smile sliding off his face. 'Na for which street the madam dey live forVoro?'

'You wan go look foram there?' Kela asked, looking serious for the first time.

'Dat no be answer,'Ahoka said, impatiently.

'I think dem mention something like Landscape Avenue.'

'You dey sure about dat?' he asked, finding it difficult to suppress the waves of excitement that surged through him.

'I dey sure,' Kela said, looking puzzled.

'Shebi, dem show the ring for television?' Ahoka asked again.

'Of course, dem showam. If they no showam how person go take know say na the ring wey dem dey find?'

'How e be?'

'Shebi, you don finam?' Kela asked, unable to contain his curiosity further.

'No, I wan begin go look foram instead of picking useless bottles around. I don begin get big,

big interest for the big money wey dey inside,' he said, patting Kela on his back.

'You think say me sef never think dat way?' Kela said, laughing again.'But, I come see say to search for the ring be like searching for needle inside Hacul beach, naim I come comot the idea for my head.'

'Never mind the wahala wey dey inside,' Ahoka said with a lot of warmth in his voice. 'Just tell me how e be and I go run off begin the search of my life.'

'Well, if you wan suffer your legs for nothing, wetin be my own for inside,' he said, shrugging his shoulders 'The ring dey very small and dem talk say na gold dem take makeam.'

'Kela the Great!' Ahoka cried, excitedly smacking Kela on his cheek. 'Here I go!' he shouted, darting off.

Like Bewudi, Kela stood staring at his back not knowing what to make of his behaviour. Finally, he shrugged his shoulders and walked back into Sefawa dunes.

Chapter Sixteen

Ahoka kept running until he got to Landscape Avenue. He was sure Madam Narosi was no other person than the fat woman he always saw whenever he was on Landscape Avenue for work; the woman with the sad brooding expression. He had avoided asking Kela the description of the woman or her house number for fear of further exciting his already excited suspicion. When he got to the street, he brought out the ring and examined it for the third time.' God!' he prayed again clasping the ring firmly in his right palm. 'Let this be the ring. 'One million rida; that is the U. S. A for me. What will I stay and do in this rotten Republic again? When I hit the jackpot there, I will come for Sindra my friend. With all the dollars in my pocket, her father can't come between us.' He put the ring back into the ragbag and started hurrying towards the fat woman's house.

Madam Narosi's watchman was at the gate when he got to the house. He was an old, withered man in a time-worn kaftan wearing a toilworn expression on his wrinkled face.

'Good afternoon papa,' Ahoka said, bowing his head.

'Wetting you come find here?' he asked, looking hostile.

'Na madam I come see,' he said more obsequious than before.

'Madam no dey,' he said still looking hostile. 'Even if she dey, who you be to wan seeyam?'

'OK, you monkey, here you get it,' he said to himself. 'You don't turn up your shrunken nose at me. Papa, I know say I be nothing just as you too be nothing, but I wan see madam,' he backchatted at the old man.

'You dey talk to me like dat?' the old man said, swinging his big stick at him. There was little steam in the swing and he easily caught the stick with one hand. He jerked the old man forward then violently pushed the stick against him. He fell on his back releasing a tight scream.

'Now, tell me where madam dey or I go close your half-witted life,' he said, viciously brooding over the old man.

'True, e no dey house,' he cried, cowering from him. 'And I no know where e go.'

'OK, I don believe you,' he said, walking away from him. 'But, if I come find say na lie you dey lie, I go come here one day cut your dirty bele the way dem dey cut chicken own, you hear me?' he said, baring his eye balls at the old man.

'I hear,' he said with a tremor in his voice. 'True, e no dey.'

'E better be true for you to continue dey wack eba,' he said, going to stand by the house's electric pole. He had not stood there for a full minute when he saw Madam Narosi's ash coloured Mercedes Benz car racing fast towards the house. Madam Narosi was behind the wheels. The car was coming so fast he was beginning to fear if she would stop by the house at all. So he brought out the ring from the ragbag and waved it in the air even as she drew close to him. The car rapidly lost speed and came to a storming halt a few metres away from him. The car door nearly came off the hinges as she flung it open in her excitement to get out of the car.

Her eyes were on the small ring Ahoka was holding between his thumb and index finger.

'Where did you find it?' she cried, leaping at the ring.

'Inside that dustbin ma,' he said breathlessly, pointing at the wastes receptacle by the gate.

'How did you find it?' she asked, excitedly, turning the ring in her palm. The joy on her fat face was something to look at.

'I found it when I came here to look for empty bottles a month or so ago. As I was rummaging for bottles inside the dustbin, I came by this small handbag,' he said, showing her the small ragbag.

'My God!' she cried. 'This is my bag. It is even worth more than the ring. It is a heirloom of our family. It is funny I don't even know it is also lost. These children will kill me one day.' She snatched the ragbag from him.

'It was inside it I found the ring,' he said.

'But, why didn't you bring it to me all this while?'
she asked, probing his face.

'Ma, just as you didn't know this bag was lost, I didn't know I have the ring with me until this afternoon.'

'Follow me into the house,' she said, climbing into the car. 'Let's go in and talk. More than talk, let's go in and eat, drink and be merry; for today I am reconciled with my dead husband.'

He was about to hop into the front seat with her when she started the engine and drove through the gate telling him with her hand to follow her.

He walked through the gate into the house's compound not quite as cheerful as a man of good fortune. The watchman who had watched and listened to him talking with his mistress, winked at him smiling. He felt like spitting on his wrinkled face, but checked the feeling.

Inside Madam Narosi's sitting-room, she flopped down on a double cushion chair and drew out a small eating stool between her cushions for him to sit on. Her two children were inside the study-room playing scrabble.

'What will you drink; water or soft drink?' she asked, the wild excitement gone from her face.

'Anything ma,' he said, his eyes taking stock of the sitting-room. The leather cushion chairs were ash coloured, so were the rug carpet, the curtains and the blinds. Even the wall painting was ash-coloured. It looked like she was in love with the ash-colour. Near one of the bedroom doors was a wine-cellar. The case for electronic gadgets stood to the left of the cellar. On the wall hung a big grandfather's clock. Tortoise shells dotted every part of the wall giving him the eerie feeling of being in a tortoise's den.

Madam Narosi went and brought a bottle of wine and 7up from the wine-cellar. She opened the7up bottle with an opener and gave it to Ahoka while she poured herself a glass of wine.

'I am very happy,' she said, taking a sip of the wine. 'Not only for myself that I now have my bag and ring back but also for you that you are now a rich man.'

'Thank you, ma,' he said, his heart beating fast.

'Where do you live?' she asked, suddenly.

'Under a bridge between Beku Island and Desowa ma,' he answered, uneasily.

'Junk Republic indeed,' she said. 'How can a complete human being live under a bridge like water?' For a moment she was quiet. From the slight twitch on her brows, it was obvious she was scheming something. 'Yes, my boy,' she said, after about two minutes of silence. 'What's your name?'

'Ahoka, ma,' he replied, still feeling uneasy.

'Fine, Ahoka,' she said, shine flowing back into her face. 'I have just done some thinking. My thinking is that since you don't have a house to live in, I will give you my boys' quarters to live in instead of the one million rida I offered as reward. Living in my boys' quarters you will work for me and I will pay you good money. I know you can easily spend the one million rida and go back to living under the bridge which is not quite a proper habitation for anybody with birth claims on homosapiens. I can assure you my boys' quarters is worth two million rida, which is twice the amount I offered as reward.'

'No, ma,' he said, his heart racing. 'I also did some thinking before running here. It is the money I want, not a house. I want to flee this rotten Republic as fast as a plane can take me to America the land of hope.'

'But, why run to America when you can stay back here and make it,' she said, shocked by his outburst. 'America is Eldorado for the whites and may be the Asians, but a sure hell for all blacks, poor or rich, educated or illiterate. There is too much racial discrimination against blacks in America. My boy, stay here with us.'

But Ahoka's mind was firmly made up against the Republic for the United States of America. America was it, America he was heading to; discrimination or no discrimination. Nothing anybody would say would change his mind. America was it, America he was heading to. That was where the brass was as Jenks would put it.

'I have heard you ma,' he said in a firm voice. 'But even here in the Republic, I have never been welcomed, not to talk of being given a chance. I have always felt like living among people worse than strangers: enemies ma. Ma, I hate the Republic.'

'My boy, don't hate the Republic,' she said in a shocked voice. 'You have been discriminated against because you have no money. But if you get the money I offered as reward or you accept to live in my boys' quarters and work for me, you will become a rich man and nobody will discriminate against you.'

'Let me think about it,' he said, not wanting to appear too adamant.

'So what do I give you now, the money or the house?' she asked after a long interval of silence.

'The money ma.'

Fine,' she said, smiling ruefully at him. She stood up and walked into one of the bedrooms.

'Ahoka's heart was beating so loudly he could hear its beating.

In a moment, she was back in the sitting room holding a black polythene bag. 'Take your money,' she said, hurling the polythene bag at him. 'There is three hundred thousand rida there for you,' she went on, looking forked out.' So you can leave for your America this very evening, if that is what you feel like.'

'But, ma, I thought you said one million rida; how do we now come by three hundred thousand?'

'What I offered and what I am giving you are two different things,' she said, going touchy. 'Besides, have you ever come by this kind of money in your street life?'

With shaky hands, he opened the polythene bag and peered at the new five hundred rida notes stacked neatly together in two rows. The moment his eyes fell on the money, all the pangs of disappointment that had just gripped him melted away. It mattered not how much he was given, he told himself, so long as it could take him to America the land of hope. He was confident the money in the polythene bag would more than take him there. There, he would pick up a job either as a cleaner or cook and work his fingers to the bone until he strikes it rich.

'Thank you, ma,' he said in a tight voice.

'Don't mention,' she said, looking bored.

Now that he had the money, he could not stay in the house a minute longer. He must get going to start preparing for his escape to America. The earlier, the better, he told himself.

'Ma, I will be on my way,' he said, getting up from the stool.

'Take care my dear,' she said, slightly raising her hand in what she considered her farewell.

'I will, ma,' he said, walking out of the house. By the gate, the watchman smiled cheerfully at him holding out his threadbare hands for a handshake.

He looked at him scornfully and walked on not stopping.

'Please, ogar, make you pity me dash me small money now,' he pleaded, slapping one hand on the other.

'I say you are a rotten son of this rotten Republic and I hate you both,' he said over his shoulder.

For no reason, a crippling fear gripped him as he approached the police checkpoint near his residence. He could not remember the number of times he had walked through this checkpoint without the police taking as much as a second look at him, not to talk of asking him *wetin he dey carry*; still he went on walking like a cat on hot bricks, the polythene bag containing the money held firmly in his right hand. A sergeant and a constable were at the checkpoint that evening. The sergeant was a fat man with an oak-like frame and a potbelly that did not make for smart movement. He had almost gone through the checkpoint when he heard the rasping voice of the fat sergeant coming from behind him. 'Hey bobo, stop there and show me wetin you dey carry for leather bag!' he said, straining himself to walk fast.

He stopped walking and stood watching the sergeant coming, the stuffing completely knocked out of him.

'Holy Mary,' the fat sergeant muttered, gaping at the new five hundred rida notes stacked inside the polythene bag. 'Shebi, you don rob the State Bank?' he asked, staring at Ahoka the way a dog would stare at a toddler holding a fat bone.

'Not on my life,' he managed to chuckle. 'Na me find Madam Narosi's ring and na the reward money be dis.'

The constable with the fat sergeant joined them. He staggered back when he saw the money, a short whistle escaping his lips. 'Na for where the gizzard tell you say him get dis kind money?' he asked the fat sergeant.

'E say naim find the lost ring wey dem dey announce every time for television and the money na the reward money,' the sergeant said, wiping sweat from his face.

'You believe dat kind yeye tori?' the constable asked.

'Yes, of course!' the fat sergeant said, winking at him with his right eye. The wink was lost on Ahoka. Already, the fat sergeant was thinking of what he would do with money. If he handled this thing well, he stood to make a double kill from one throw. He would have the money and get promoted to the rank of Inspector of Police if he could hand Ahoka over as a houseboy who had killed his master and was attempting to run away. If he was given the promised monetary reward by the government, which he doubted, that would be fine. If he was not given the money, which he believed would be the case, at least he would have Ahoka's money to fall back on.

'Gizzard on your way,' the constable said, smiling slyly at Ahoka. 'You be lucky gizzard, chappie boy.'

He walked on for about a hundred metres then left the express road for the small path that would bring him to his residence. Somewhere down the path, he had an uneasy feeling of someone following him, but dismissed it as the feeling he usually experienced whenever he walked through a lonely place especially the small cemetery between Beku Island and Voro. Neither Bewudi nor his wife were at home when he got to the bridge. Their household effects were also gone. It looked like they had packed and fled the bridge.

He went and tucked the money into their aluminium pot, then turned the pot over with the money inside. He ran to the lagoon to have a quick bath before leaving the bridge for good that day. He swam far into the lagoon before swimming back to shore. He scrubbed his body with a worn-out sponge then washed himself clean. He slipped into his trousers and ran up the bridge. Out of joy and anxiety, he went to check his money. He turned up the pot, and a powdery substance poured out of the polythene bag. The money was gone. He gave a choking scream then fainted. He came to some thirty minutes later to find the fat sergeant and the constable bending over him.

'Wake up gizzard,' the constable said, pinching one of his toes.

'No, I wan die,' he cried, rolling away from them. 'Dem don tif my money wetin I wan live for?'

'If na die you wan die, na for prison you go die no be here,' the sergeant said, mopping his fat face with a dirty handkerchief.

'My money, my money!' he cried, hitting his head on the bridge concrete. Blood started spurting out of his forehead.

'Dis bobo don go bananas finish,' the sergeant said, shocked by Ahoka's suicide attempts. 'Carryam for shoulder, let's begin go station,' he ordered the constable.

It seemed the constable did not like the task his senior was saddling him with for he remained standing where he was.

'No be you I dey talk to?' The sergeant blared.

The constable took two steps towards Ahoka then stopped. Ahoka was fast drifting into a coma from lost of blood and extreme anxiety.

'I no wan sleep for bridge,' the sergeant said in a quiet, sinister voice.

The constable finished the remaining steps between him and Ahoka and heaved him up onto his shoulder.

'Oyah, on our way,' the sergeant said, waving the constable forward with his baton.

The constable walked past him with blood dripping on his gray uniform.

The sergeant fell into steps behind him, grinning wolfishly to himself.

Chapter Seventeen

Ahoka gradually opened his eyes and saw himself lying on a bed with white bedsheet. He was covered with another white bedsheet up to his neck. A nurse was standing close to his feet scribbling something in a folder containing blue sheets of paper. He knew he was in hospital, but did not know how he arrived there. From his bed, he could see about fifteen patients lying on bare mats on the floor. It appeared there were only two beds in the ward containing about eighteen patients, and that was his own bed and that of another patient to his right. He wondered why they had been given this preference over other patients. He was later to learn the two of them were brought to the hospital by the police as property of the Republican government. He tried to lift up his head from the pillow, but a stabbing pain shot through him making him cry out.

'Sorry my dear,' the nurse said, placing her hand on his forehead which was heavily bandaged. 'Don't move again and you will be alright. Do you need some water to drink?'

He shook his head.

'Who brought me here?' he asked, grinding his teeth to sail over the nagging pain he felt near his forehead.

'Don't talk,' the nurse said. 'Talking means more pain.'

'But I want to know, ma,' he said muddle-headed.

'Well, if you insist,' the nurse said. 'But I can't see what good it will do you.'

'I want to know ma.'

The police,' she said.

'What did they say happened to my head?' he asked, trying with little success to recollect how he came by his injuries.

'According to them,' the nurse said, looking tenderly at him, 'you are a cocaine addict and you wanted to blast your head to pieces when they could not allow you to have a fix from the cocaine wraps they retrieved from you. Now please tell me the truth, are you a junkie?'

'I don't know what that means, ma.'

'I mean do you sniff or smoke such hard drugs like cocaine or marijuana?'

'Not on my life,' he said, beginning to breathe heavily.

'I never believed them a second,' she said, looking at him with more affection than before. 'You are simply not the type. Junkies rave for fixes when they come to; you haven't yet. This, however, leaves us with the question of why you wanted to blast your head to bits. Can you remember why or did somebody do it to you?'

He closed his eyes trying to remember, but whenever he got near to recollection, some unidentifiable thought would flow into his mind blocking his memory. The effort made sweat to start running down his face.

'Forget it if you can't remember,' the nurse said, fanning him with a magazine. 'The important thing is to get well, not how you became sick.'

Then he burst out, 'my money! my money! Dem don tif my money!'

The nurse was so startled by this sudden outburst that she dropped the folder and jumped back into a small locker standing behind her. She and the locker went over crashing to the floor.

'I wan my money! The money wey madam give me,' he went on crying at the top of his voice. Other patients looked at him from their mats on the floor and started yelling at the ward attendants. 'Why did you bring a lunatic into this ward, or do you think we are all lunatics and this is a madhouse?'

The nurse struggled to her feet and ran out of the ward. A moment later, she was back with a doctor and the fat Sergeant.

'My money! My money! I wan my money!' he cried again and again.

'Which money the gizzard dey talk about?' the sergeant asked, blustering into the ward.

'How on earth will I know?' the nurse said with an angry expression on her face.

'Yeah, you no go know,' the sergeant said with a hangdog look on his face. On their way to the police station with Ahoka, the constable had suddenly said, 'but dis boy be like the boy

Inspector Onisuru arrested for the murder of Okime and him family, but Jakore releasam?'

The fat sergeant nearly had a heartattack. Twice he had the feeling of having seen Ahoka elsewhere than on the road, but could not say where. The constable's suggestion has now told him where. If only he would take less alcohol and hard drugs, his memory would serve him better he thought. He could now vividly recollect how he and the constable saw Inspector Onisuru and Ahoka upon the latter's arrival at police headquarters in Joko town and what Onisuru had said concerning Ahoka's involvement in the massacre of Okime and his family. He could also remember how two days later, Onisuru had told him how Jakore had punctured his allegations against Ahoka and released the boy.'Stop, stop!' he commanded the constable.

The constable stopped walking.

'Put him down.'

Ahoka was laid on the ground.

The fat sergeant beamed his torchlight on his face. Whatever doubt he had before was now removed. Hot sweat started pouring all over his face. What a big fool he would have made of himself if he had made the charge he was proposing against Ahoka and Jakore got to hear of it? 'Na since when you begin think say dis boy be the same boy Onisuru bring for station the other day?' he asked the constable, mopping his face.

'Na just now the thought jump into my mind,' the constable said, happy his hunch had turned out to be correct.' Wetin we go do now?'

'We go killam throwey the bodi for lagoon,' the fat sergeant said, unslinging his gun.

The constable's heart started beating violently. He would stand for anything but murder. No, he won't go along with this. Besides, if Ahoka was killed, he would be the one to carry the dead body back to the lagoon. No, he could not stand this. But what was he to do to stop the fat sergeant from carrying out his intention. The fat sergeant was a vicious man that would stop at nothing to get what he wanted; that included killing him along with Ahoka if it came to that. Sweat dropped off his face.

The fat sergeant was already pointing his gun at Ahoka, his index finger curling round the trigger.

'Wetin you go say happen to the bullets dem give you for office?' the constable asked the fat sergeant in panic.

'No be their bullet I go use,' the fat sergeant said. 'I dey carry my own bullets.'

'Na from where you get bullets?' the constable asked, alarmed by this declaration. Who him dey work with? he wondered, fearfully.

'Where I dey get my bullets no be your concern,' the fat sergeant said and looked to his right. A police van had just parked on the other side of the road and two policemen where walking towards where they were.

The constable heaved a sigh of relief.

The fat sergeant was gripped by fear and anger. But he soon got a second wind. There was no problem. There would always be a way out. 'Dis junkie na wa o foram!' he said loudly and reeled with laughter as the other two policemen came to stand in front of him.

The constable was shocked speechless. Dis man na wa o for you, he thought. How one man go get so many bad ideas for him head?

'Wetin, dis one dey smoke?' one of the two policemen that just came asked.

'Dis one no be smoke him dey smoke, na sniff e dey sniff and e be like cocaine e dey sniff my broda,' the fat sergeant said in a more buoyant spirit than before. Who said he would not prosecute this guy and may be get promoted for it? 'See the stuff we recover for him hand,' he said, producing from his pocket a powdery substance wrapped in a piece of paper.

The other two policemen did not even bother to look at the substance he was showing them as they turned back and headed for their vehicle. 'See you for station tomorrow!' one of them said on their way to the van on the other side of the road. The constable was yet to fully recover his shocked wits.

Ahoka began to emit a frightening noise from his nose that was sounding like death throes. The fat sergeant ran after the other policemen telling them to stop and help him take the junkie to hospital as he was about dying. Together with the constable, the fat sergeant carried Ahoka to the police van across the road. The van took off for Gojukwe University Teaching Hospital.

After depositing Ahoka at the hospital, the fat sergeant went and made arrangements of charging him to court with the Judge of the court he had in mind and the state counsel that would prosecute the case. What he wanted was a quick trial that would not last more than a week or at most two weeks. Every day he came to the hospital to see if Ahoka was fit for trial. He was sitting outside the ward when Ahoka started wailing about his money.

'My money, my money!' Ahoka cried again, getting more restless.

'Easy, easy,' the doctor said, placing his hand on Ahoka's stomach. 'The more you cry, the more the pain. Just be quiet and tell me about this money you are talking about.'

'But the bobo don craze finish,' the sergeant said, a somewhat frightened expression on his face. 'You no go rely on a junkie to talk sense?'

'But he doesn't look to me like one who takes grass,' the doctor said. 'A guy who smokes grass stinks a mile; this boy doesn't. Besides, cocaine cost big money; where will a poor boy like this find the money to buy cocaine?'

'But dis na the stuff we recover for him hand,' the sergeant said, showing them a powdery substance in a polythene bag.' 'Either e be sniffer or e be pusher and all na the same thing.'

For a moment the doctor stood staring at the powdery substance not saying anything. The nurse sat down on the small locker looking passionately at Ahoka.

'My money! My money!' he cried again, kicking his legs.

'I say be quiet,' the doctor said, getting exasperated. 'Which money are you talking about?'

'The money madam give me,' he said, calming down.

'Which madam?'

He closed his eyes trying to remember Madam Narosi's name, again his memory failed him and he blacked out.

'See wetin I mean about a junkie wey don go bananas?' the sergeant said, beaming with smiles. 'E go dey speak junk, no sense at all.'

'I think what he needs is a good rest,' the doctor said, talking to the nurse. 'May be later in the day, he would be sober and in good command of his memory.'

'We hope so sir,' the nurse said, standing up. The three filed out of the ward with the doctor leading the way and the fat sergeant bringing up the rear.

'But ogar doctor,' the sergeant said as they came out of the ward to the corridor.

The doctor stopped and looked at him.

'Ye, sergeant, anything?'

'No be something wey concern you sir,' he said, rubbing his head with his right hand. 'I only wan tell una, we wan chargeam to court tomorrow for sniffing and trafficking in hard drugs and narcotics.'

'But that should be after his recovery,' the nurse said, looking hostile.

'No be so madam,' the sergeant said. 'But when e go fit walka by himself.'

'Whatever you choose to call it,' the doctor said, moving towards his office.

The fat sergeant smirked at him, turned and walked out of the hospital.

Chapter Eighteen

'C-o-u-r-t!' Ahoka heard the court clerk calling as the judge made his entrance into the courtroom. Every body including Ahoka stood up. The judge bowed and sat down. The bar and the public gallery also bowed and sat down.

'Yes,' the judge said, looking like a man carved out of marble. 'How many matters do we have on the Cause List today?'

'Eight, your lordship,' the court clerk said. He went on to call them. Ahoka's case was second on the list. The judge said he would take only the first two matters while lawyers in the other cases could take new dates.

The court clerk a reverend gentleman stood up again and called the first case on the list. The parties came out and lawyers announced their appearances. Court proceedings had begun.

Ahoka sat on his seat reviewing the chain of events that led to his being in court that day. The whole thing started with Madam Narosi giving him money for finding her ring. He carried the money home and tucked it into a pot. Some moments later, he returned from the lagoon to find the money gone and in its place was a powdery substance. He started screaming and then all went blank for him. When he came to later, two policemen were hovering over him. Then he started knocking his head on the bridge concrete crying for his money. Again, he blacked out. Later, he woke up to find himself in hospital with a nurse standing beside his bed. She and a doctor wanted to know who gave him the money he was crying about but he could not remember Madam Narosi's name nor other details of the reward before going into a coma again. When he finally regained consciousness, he was in a fit condition to remember Madam Narosi's name and other details of the reward. But the police insisted he was a junkie and a pusher who could not be relied upon to talk sense. The doctor and the nurse insisted Madam Narosi be contacted to verify his story, but unfortunately she had flown out of the country on a three months intensive medical treatment abroad. With no one to confirm his claims, he was left with only his own words, which the police insisted were those of a junkie. Accordingly, they went on to frame two count charges of sniffing and pushing cocaine against him.

For two weeks, he was remanded in police custody before being brought to court. He and other suspects were brought out of police custody into a waiting Black Maria around 8.30 am with the hope of getting to court before 9 am the court's sitting time. They actually got to court in good time, but the judge did not start sitting till 12.30 pm. According to the court Registrar, he was in his chambers attending to weightier matters. Sitting on the accused bench, he watched lawyers putting questions to witnesses while the judge scribbled away.

When he was still in school, his teacher Mr Binda Kiama, once told him that all the judges of the Republic were merchandise for money and fear and they gave their judgement as they were persuaded by either or both. The government dangled the fear of compulsory retirement or continuous lack of promotion over their heads while the rich enticed them with money.

According to him, he once had a court case with one of the sharks in Beku. A big plot of land was left for him by his deceased father as inheritance. One day, he woke up to find a big fence erected around the land and houses in different stages of completion. The following day, he was in court to file an action for trespass, damages and injunction. When the matter finally came before the court for hearing, judgement was entered for the shark against him. As one of his reasons for giving judgement to the shark, the judge held that he was guilty of laches and acquiescence and equity, aids only the vigilant, not the indolent. What was more, his lordship added, buildings such as those erected by the shark enhanced the beauty of Beku. He wanted to appeal but his relations advised him not to as the appeal was likely to be an echo of the first judgement. Worse, he did not even have the means of prosecuting an appeal.

Sitting in the courtroom, he wondered whether he would end up like Binda Kiama: a victim of the decayed and corrupt judiciary of the Republic.

'Yes, next case,' the judge said, reclining back on his chair after disposing the first case.

The court clerk stood up and called Ahoka's case. He stood up and walked to the accused stand. After pleading not guilty to the two count charges leveled against him, proceedings began once more. He could not afford the services of a lawyer and the court did not provide him with one. So he had to conduct his defence himself.

The prosecution opened its case by calling on the Investigation Police Officer, the fat sergeant, as the first prosecution witness. He went to the witness box and swore by the Bible to tell the truth, the whole truth and nothing but the truth. He went on to testify to the effect that he and one Constable Tonga were on night patrol around Beku Island and Desowa areas when they came upon Ahoka by Menda junction sniffing cocaine. On sighting them, he attempted throwing away the small wrap containing the cocaine, but they were too fast for him. Seeing he was a junkie or something near that, they forced him to take them to his abode with the hope of recovering more of the stuff from him. Their visit paid off. The prosecution then sought to tender the powdery substance the fat sergeant claimed to have recovered from Ahoka as an exhibit. It was so tendered, admitted and marked 'Exhibit AA" without the judge asking for an objection from Ahoka or inquiring from the prosecution whether the necessary forensic tests and their procedures had been complied with.

After the close of the prosecution's case, the judge looked at Ahoka grimly and said,'yes, accused person, what have you to say in your defence?'

He began by stating how he had found Madam Narosi's lost ring; how she gave him the money and how he returned from the lagoon later that day to find the money gone and in its place, a powdery substance he knew nothing about. He went on to state how the police later descended on him accusing him of sniffing and pushing cocaine, and gave lucid evidence of his belief that the police stole his money and put the powdery substance in the polythene bag. He closed his case by giving evidence of the fruitless efforts that were made to get Madam Narosi to confirm his story.

The case was adjourned for three days for the judge to write his judgement. On the day of judgement, Ahoka was brought to court by 8.55 am, but the court did not sit till 11 am. The judge directed the court clerk to call Ahoka's case first being the only case for judgemen that day. After the case was called and the prosecuting state counsel announced his appearance, the judge cleared his throat and began to read his judgement. While stating the case made out by the prosecution, the judge went on a trip of judicial eloquence lacing his words with poetic juices. In the end, he held that the prosecution had proved its case beyond reasonable doubt. As for the defence, the judge held thatAhoka had woefully failed to offer any defence to any of the two count charges levelled against him and as such, he had been found guilty of sniffing and trafficking in cocaine and narcotics as charged. The case was not one of pleading *allocutus* the judge further held. Ahoka is hereby sentenced to ten years imprisonment with hard labour.

Immediately the judge pronounced the sentence, a shrill cry was heard coming from the public gallery. The judge jumped backward on his seat, his eye glasses falling off. The facade of judicial neutrality and blindness was gone. It looked like his lordship was afraid.

Ahoka spun round on the accused stand where he was standing to see Sindra advancing on his lordship from the front exit door, a small pistol held firmly in her right hand while tears flowed freely on her cheeks. He was shocked beyond words. From where did she spring up? He was sure she was not in the courtroom when he was giving evidence. He was not even sure she was around when the case was adjourned to this day. From where did she spring up then?

For about twenty seconds, there was complete silence in the courtroom. Nobody moved. Sindra kept moving nearer his lordship with the mouth of the pistol centred on his forehead.

'I want this judgement changed,' she said, her voice trembling.

'If you say so ma, if you say so,' the judge said in a voice that shared little with his earlier eloquent voice.

'I say so,' she said, looking at him contemptuously.

'Yes, ma, yes ma,' he said, picking up his Ball-Point pen. Then from nowhere the fat sergeant knocked Sindra from the rear sending her somersaulting forward. The gun exploded with a bang and the whole courtroom was thrown into confusion with women shrieking and screaming.

'Your lordship's judgement dey kankpe!' the fat sergeant cried amidst the confusion. 'The gizzard dey him way to Jaruwa prison while the bitch go wait for the punishment wey my lord go giveam!'

'You have spoken sergeant,' his lordship said, coming from under his table, sweat all over his face. 'You are a Daniel come to Judgement!'

Chapter Nineteen

In the same cell with Ahoka in Jaruwa prison was an elderly man with an unkempt moustache and an equally unkempt beard that had gone grey. Ahoka put his age at about sixty. Although he appeared to be aging fast, the look on his face was that of a vicious gangster possessed by a voracious urge of maiming, killing and devouring. For the first two weeks that Ahoka spent in the prison, he never saw him talking to anybody even when spoken to. He sat still while his face changed from one vicious snarl to another. One day as they were being taken out to work on one of the prison farms, he suddenly jumped on one of the prison warders knocking him against the prison wall. The warder's head hit the wall and he slid to the ground, his eyes rolling. The man fell on top of him biting him everywhere. All the other inmates stood watching their faces going ashen. It took the combined efforts of three warders to tear him off the fallen warder. For two days, the prison authorities instructed the leader of his cell, known as the *Baskethead* by his fellow inmates, not to give him any food. The *Baskethead* in charge of sharing food to inmates of his cell carried out this instruction with faithfulness that suggested malice or vengeance. But the man's face showed no sign of penitence. Instead, he kept swearing to himself and banging his fist on the wall. On the third day, food was given to him on instruction by the prison authorities. For a long time, he sat staring at the food doing nothing. Then he stood up, urinated on the food, then kicked it viciously over.

WhenAhoka saw this, he became afraid. 'What sort of man is this?' he wondered. After a long while, he ventured to ask him, 'papa why you no wan chop? For three days now, you never chop; please chop papa.'

He turned and looked at Ahoka then gave him a faint smile. 'Make you no wori about me my pikin,' he said in a tight voice. 'Shebi, if I die I no go chop dem pig-wash again?'

His smile did things to Ahoka in the sordid prison world where smiles and laughter were affairs of dreams.

'Please, make you no die papa,' he said in an emotion-laden voice.' Begin chop. Wetin man go do as e don come enter dis hole?'

'My pikin,' he said with a vacant expression on his face.'No be because I dey dis dirty hole naim dey make me no wan chop dem pigwash, but na vex wan kill me as dem no wan allow our kingdom come.'

'Which kingdom?' Ahoka asked, looking confused.

The man gave him a faint, dry smile and remained quiet for sometime, his eyes on him. He seemed to be debating in his mind whether or not he was the sort of person he could repose confidence in. Finally, he shrugged his shoulders and said, 'the tori na long tori my pikin and na

154

because of dat tori I dey here. 1 go begin nackam to you by telling you my name and the suffer, suffer wey my legs and bele don suffer for dis we obodo Republic.' He paused and ran him over with his eyes once more then went on. 'My name na Biyaku. I be pikin of a Reverend Father from the east. I come dis Beku wey I still be small pikin to find job. No where wey I never look for job, but I never finam. The yeye people go always ask me to bring certificate as if na certificate go work. I never find job, I never see chop. Some days wey bele go pepe me, na market I dey go taste *gari* as if I wan buyam. Later, I go go back drink water for my house under Tonka bridge.'

Again, there was an interval of silence as Biyaku paused and stared at Ahoka trying to make up his mind whether to go on with his story or stop there. 'How old you be?' he asked Ahoka, finally.

'As my papa tell me, I be nineteen years old now,' he said, looking curiously at the man.

'I see, which kind work dat your papa dey do?'

'When e still dey with me, na watchman e be for one shark house for Beku Island.'

'When e still dey with you,' Biyaku repeated nodding his head. 'Wetin dat mean?' His face was alive with interest.

"I no wan talk about dat again,' Ahoka said, looking sad and sorrowful.

'But I be papa to you,' Biyaku pleaded. 'If you no fit tell me something, who you go tellam in dis hole?'

He looked into Biyaku's eyes and saw the fire of anxiety and enthusiasm burning there, then began: 'As I don tell you, my papa be watchman for one big man house for Beku Island. About five months ago, e go work but never return. As I no seeyam for house, I walka go Okime's house where e be watchman. But wetin I find? Okime with all him pikins plus wife dem dey dead inside dem own blood. Assassins don bucha them all. But dat no be my wori. Person wey chop him share come chop poor man own put no suppose die better death. My wori na for my papa. No place wey police no search for dat house, but they no seeyam. No place wey I never carry my leg reach for dis Beku dey look foram, but I never seeyam. Even as I dey talk to you, I never seeyam since e carry him leg comot our domot dat day. Whether e still dey breathe or e don decay finish for Hacul beach and lagoon dem, na only God sabi.'

'Make you never wori your head again,' Biyaku said with a mischievous smile. 'Your papa dey kankpe and helele for Mermaid Shell.'

'Why you dey take talk concerning my papa play?' Ahoka asked, bitterly. The relief he felt after telling Biyaku the sorrow that sat heavily on his chest left him. 'Where Mermaid Shell dey? Who takeam there?' he asked, a strange kind of anger he had never felt before gripping him. It was anger tampered by fear and respect for the person against whom it was directed and hope in what he had to say.

'The tori na long one,' Biyaku said, the smile sliding off his face. 'And na because of dat tori I dey here. As sharks and the President their friend get *Club de Gallery Human de Vampirists* for inside Beku Island, na so we poor people come get *Mermaid Shell* for Riakere rocks between Beku and Harkowa. And as sharks dey sit down dey plan how dem go continue dey suck poor man blood, na so poor men dey tanda dey learn how dem go swallow sharks and dem sea inside Mermaid Shell.'

Wetin you dey talk?' Ahoka asked, paralysed with fear.

'You no go understand until I tell you the whole tori,' Biyaku said, a benign expression on his face. 'Just get small patience.'

He said nothing as he sat staring at Biyaku, fear and anxiety wailing in him.

'As I don dey tell you.' Biyaku said, looking poised for a long tale. 'I walka Beku for many years, I no see job, I no see chop. One day, I come see say man pikin must help himself as neither God nor gofmen fit saveam. So I run go meet Welema for Sindika wey I don hear say e dey give gun. I giveam the money wey dey my pocket and e give me gun, I come run to one petrol station show them the gun and dem pack the whole money wey dey the petrol station give me for hand. E dey dat easy my pikin. As I dey operate for Beku, I come jam Jokulo wey come from north. Him too come tell me say e come Beku find job but e never seeyam. My pikin, make you no think say Jokulo be like me and you,' he went on after a momentary pause. 'E sabi book well, well. With my korokoro eyes, I take see him two degrees wey e carry for pocket dey chase job for Beku. But na so e walka with plenty degrees for pocket and plenty book for head, but e never smell job. As big men wey dey give job dey ask me to show them certificate na so dem dey ask him to give them kola. As e never get kola to give or long leg to walka reach where job dey, e never finam. One evening, e return from Khiro where e go find job for one of the big merchant banks there to find him broda wife wey e dey stay with crying. E asksam wetin happen and e tellam say gofmen don sack him broda for the ministry wey him dey work sake of say too many workers dey the ministry. E never know when him begin cry join the woman. Even when him broda dey work, the salary wey him dey collect fit give them only one meal. Now dat him job don leaveam, dat one meal don kuku leave them join be dat. Dat same evening as e dey sit down for verandah him bele dey makeam see double, the pikin of one Army General drive passam for brown V-boot Mercedes Benz car throwing mud for him bodi. As if dat never do, the boy inside the car lookam for inside driving mirror and begin laugh. Dat day, Jokulo feel like killing himself as e lie down for bed anger choking him neck and hunger making him bele to sing noisy songs. E come see say the suffer wey e dey suffer no be because e never work hard to get job, but because gofmen and big men dem wey corner job no wan giveam chance to enjoy the life wey God giveam. E come see say to enjoy dat life, e must get the Republic hold for hand. Then e go establish him own kingdom. Dat kingdom him go call Lucifer's kingdom. But as e dey fight for the coming of dat kingdom e go callam tomorrow's kingdom; and the fight for dat kingdom e go call exorcism.

The following day, e run go meet Welema who giveam gun. From dat day e begin fight for the coming of tomorrow's kingdom. In dat kingdom according to Jokulo, every man go dey chop as e get power. If you no get power, you go die for hunger. Na gun go rule for dat kingdom not the stupid, weak biro wey send me and you to dis hole; wey dey make weak people dey chop and strong people dey die for hunger. And e go comot rich men bele wey don chop dem share come chop poor man's own add. E go drive them comot dis world put for another. Dis one na proper exorcism for sharks dem my pikin. Me I see sense with Jokulo.'

'But me, no be all dis I wan hear,' Ahoka said, butting into Biyaku's long tale. 'Na how my papa take dey the place you dey call Mermaid Shell I wan know; wetin be my own for Lucifer's kingdom or Devil's kingdom?'

'I go tell you how e come take him leg enter Mermaid Shell,' Biyaku said, hastily. 'Just cool down small, allow me tell you the whole tori.'

'I dey listen,' Ahoka said, looking restless.

'You see, even as I never go school,' Biyaku said, licking his dry lips. 'I get sense small, small. I know say na two things dey rule dis our yeye world and if e go end as.my old papa dey cryam for inside him church, na one of dis things go enam. Dis two things na gun and biro. Now na biro dey rule. Naim make me and you poor. Naim make some people dey live for Beku Island and others for Desowa. So in dis yeye world, man must choose which side e go dey: gun side or biro side. Me I don choose gun side; not because I no sabi book, but because 1 know say biro be weak thing and e go soon die and gun go take over.' He coughed and then went on. 'I happy as I meet you here a young and clever boy for west. After we don leave dis dirty hole, you go go lead exorcism for east, and I go go leadam for north. Jokulo go continue dey leadam for west inside Mermaid Shell. Dat way, we go dey kill not knowing papa or mama, uncle or auntie, broda or sista. We all go fight for the coming of tomorrow's kingdom: Lucifer's kingdom. Now I don come to where and how your papa come enter Mermaid Shell,' he said, his voice slightly rising.

Ahoka leaned forward taking his cheeks in his palms.

'As Jokulo come dey fight for tomorrow's kingdom,' Biyaku continued, 'e come see say him alone no go fit drive away all the obelente bele people wey boku for dis Republic; e come change plan. Him new plan be say, e go get other poor

160

people to helpam. Na so e come jam me, na so e come jam your papa. E jam me for Voro the very week wey dem tif my gun under Tonka bridge. As I no get gun, I no kuku get chop. For three days, I come dey work for one big man for Voro sake of say e go pay me money make I run go meet Welema again. But no money come as the man no gree pay. On the third day wey me and other two men dey cut grass for the man house, naim Jokulo jam us.'

'Shebi na die you wan make I die before you go tell me about my papa?' Ahoka butted in again, shaking with impatience and anxiety. 'How long I go sit here dey listen to your long, long tori?'

'Make you no die my fine, fine pikin,' he said in a soft, wooing voice. 'I go tell you now. As 1 don dey tell you, Jokulo see say e need men wey go dey helpam swallow the plenty, plenty sharks wey full dis Republic, e begin kill the sharks dey take dem servants dey put for Mermaid Shell. Now you don see how your papa come take beautiful style enter Mermaid Shell?' he said leaning forward to bang his fist on the wall.

'You mean say Jokulo kill Okime and him family come carry my papa put for him prison?' Ahoka cried

'Mermaid Shell no be prison,' Biyaku said, reverting to type: wild, ruthless, savage. 'I sure say e dey happy there than for inside him shack for Okime's house,' he went on scarcely above a whisper.

The expression on his face made Ahoka to shrink back into one comer of the cell.

Chapter Twenty

Biyaku was telling the truth only in a limited sense when he said he was in Jaruwa prison because of his involvement in exorcism for the coming of tomorrow's kingdom. If the authorities of the Republic had suspected he was one way or the other remotely connected with the butchery of the rich, he would have been castrated before being hanged without the necessity of a trial. The truth was that he was caught sneaking away with some foodstuff he had lifted from the store of a market woman. Under torture by the police, he admitted stealing them. But no torture could make him disclose where he was taking them. But all other things he had told Ahoka were true. There was a place known as Mermaid Shell; there was a man known as Jokulo who had suffered all Biyaku said he had suffered and was doing all Biyaku said he was doing. It was also true that Ahoka's father was in Mermaid Shell.

Mermaid Shell as Jokulo and his men called their hideout was situated deep inside Riakere rocks some thirty kilometres away from the outskirts of Beku. It was a very big tunnel measuring about sixty to sixty-five feet wide and seventy to seventy-eight feet long. It was dug by the Wajuwan soldiers during the Wajuwan War of Salvation. Jokulo and his men had further enlarged it to such extent that it could accommodate two hundred to two hundred and fifty men. Jokulo and two of his bosom friends and university colleagues called Barau and Yegama were the first to arrive the tunnel with their few belongings some seven months back. They immediately set about removing small boulders that had fallen into the tunnel and covering its big mouth with tree branches leaving only a small opening as the entrance door. Two days later, Jokulo was returning to the tunnel from Beku where he had gone to buy some foodstuff for their upkeep when he ran into Biyaku and two other men called Rawka and Haman mowing down grasses with cutlasses by the house of the former minister of finance. It was one of those sunny days in Beku when the hot tropical sun visits hell on the living. Their bodies were glistening with sweat as their dead beaten hands went up and down mowing the grasses.

Jokulo stopped and greeted them. He had in his right hand a big polythene bag containing *gari* and *agidi* flour and in his right hand *akara* and fried yam wrapped in a paperback.

Biyaku who was the most elderly of the three men dropped his cutlass and replied the greeting. The other two went on with their work as if they had not heard him.

'Papa, I get plenty *akara* and fried yam for inside dis paperback, you go like chopam?' Jokulo asked Biyaku, raising his voice high.

'How empty bele go refuse food?' Biyaku said already walking towards him.

At the mention *of akara* and fried yam, Rawka and Haman dropped their cutlasses and stood up smiling hopefully at Jokulo. Their behavior reminded Jokulo of a story his friend told him. His friend went to a house local liquor was sold. The house was filled with drunks some of whom were sitting outside the house. When his friend walked past the drunks sitting outside the house, none of them greeted him or even showed sign of having seen him. Inside the house, he bought beer and asked that it be shared to all the drunks inside and outside the house. As soon as the beer got to the drunks outside the house, a drunk outside called out to Jokulo's friend whether he heard his greeting when he was entering the house.

'Fine papa,' Jokulo said, giving Biyaku his charming smile. 'I get plenty *akara* and yam here wey you go chop beleful even remain small. Come sit down for dis shade begin wackam,' he said, moving towards a small shade provided by a small tree by the roadside.

Biyaku followed him to the shade and crouched down before the paperback Jokulo had placed on the ground.

Rawka and Haman stood in the sun, their smiles fast fading.

'Make una come chop witham now,' Jokulo said beckoning them at the same time. 'Plenty *akara* and yam dey inside the paperback, and if e no do una I go buy more.'

Rawka and Haman raced to the shade and squatted down beside Biyaku.

'You nko, you no go chop?' Biyaku asked Jokulo between mouthful.

'No, I don beleful already,' Jokulo replied amiably. 'Make una no mind me. If dis one no do una, tell me, I go buy more for una.'

'You be good pikin o,' Biyaku said, looking up at him. 'I no know say good pikins still dey dis we obodo Republic.'

The other two did not say anything. They seemed too famished for words.

'No mention papa,' Jokulo said. 'Dis one na small thing. If God know say one eye no go help the other to dey kuku see well, or one hand no go wash the other, e for make them one, one. Make you no wori papa.'

'Na wa o,' Biyaku said, obviously thrilled by what Jokulo had said. 'Which kind pikin you be sef wey dey talk pass him age?'

'Make you no wori papa. I go tell you who I be after you don chop beleful,' Jokulo said. 'Chop first.'

After they had finished eating, Jokulo learned that for the past three days, they had been in front of that house sweating out their strengths to nought. Each day, the minister's wife complained of lack of time to sign a cheque for their payment. When they had finished recounting their woes, he went on to tell them about himself, his own woes and his present plan to reverse not only his own fortunes but those of the majority poor. He concluded by saying he has all the arsenals that would give fruition to his plans in his scabbard having gone to see Welema who assured him of continuous supply of fire arms. All he needed were like-minded men of vision estranged by the corrupt and hostile socio-economic set-up in the Republic.

There and then, the three men swore they were ready to fight and if need be die for the cause of tomorrow's kingdom. According to them, they had nothing to lose by the demise of the Republic, but everything to gain by the arrival of tomorrow's kingdom. From there, they did not even go back to the places they called their homes, but followed Jokulo to Mermaid Shell.

Chapter Twenty-One

Inside Mermaid Shell, Jokulo explained to his five disciples the guiding principles and philosophy of tomorrow's kingdom and the thorny path to that kingdom. According to him, *Tomorrow's kingdom: Lucifer's kingdom*, is going to be a kingdom of the poor, run by the poor, for the good of the poor. The present oppressive rule of tyranny and exploitation would only be happenings of history to be researched into by intellectual egg-heads. A situation where sharks and government functionaries go frolicking in posh cars and boosting foreign economies with fat accounts of money stolen from the Republic's purse while the majority poor are left in a limbo would only be seen in nightmares but never in real life in the kingdom. The central philosophy of the kingdom from which government policies and actions would issue would be justice,' he stressed. 'Justice,' according to him, 'is when you work hard and you are paid or otherwise rewarded commensurate to your sweat. There is also justice where you have the qualification for a job and it is given to you on the level without a wink here or there or *a where-is-my-chop* language. There is no justice where you labour the breath out of your life only to be rewarded with peanuts. There is also no justice where you have the qualification for a job, but it goes through your fingers because you have no long legs. In tomorrow's kingdom,' he pontificated, 'if you labour the breath out of your life and you are not paid according to your sweat, shoot your employer. This way, there would be no more sweated labour nor sweatshops. If you have all the certificates in your pocket and you are denied employment because somebody has longer legs, shoot whoever is in charge of employment. If you are hungry, but have no money, enter any restaurant and order food. If the restaurant proprietor refuses you, shoot. So if you are hungry, you would be hungry only because you can't pull a gun fast. This is where the gun and the dragon come into exorcism: the war for tomorrow's kingdom,' he disclosed. 'The dragon represents the ferocity and gallantry of exorcism while the gun would give voice to that ferocity and gallantry. But after the victory of exorcism, the dragon would drop out leaving the gun to perpetuate the noble ideals of the kingdom. For this reason, every citizen of the kingdom shall be a knight during exorcism and a sheriff thereafter. As a sheriff, he would move about with his gun seeing that his rights are not abused and fearing to abuse the rights of others. These are the good tidings of tomorrow's kingdom!' he cried excitedly. 'But, first, the strategy of bringing it to pass.'

'The strategy, the strategy!' they all cried, excitement rising to a feverish point.

'Yes, the strategy!' he cried, looking even more excited than his men. 'In the strategy lies the soul of the kingdom; in it lies the hope of all sidewalkers; but more important than all these, in it lies the doom of all sharks and their Republic. My strategy is this: We start by releasing the dragon on all sharks be they in Beku or wherever in the Republic, a shark is a shark, voracious in character and oppressive in constitution. This is proper exorcism for the kingdom fellow knights. For this, I recognise we need more men. The six of us cannot ride on all the sharks spanning the length and breadth of the Republic. For days, I have thought of how to raise more men but always drew a blank. I know for certain that we cannot go to the streets like the king's servants calling on all men to come to our banquet of grapeshots. We can be sure that not too many people would be eager to be in our banquet hall. But I went on thinking. Then one day I asked myself, apart from myself and other like-minded poor men on the street who I cannot by sight know to be like-minded, but who are clearly far from the shark, are there men close to the shark who so much hate him as to be better off with him dead, and who I can with certainty know to hold such feelings against him? If there are, who are they? Are they his friends, his distant relations, his wife, his children? All these seem to me unlikely. For how can the baboon be happy at the funeral of the monkey? Then who are these people if there are? And there they were: his servants of course! Who else? Apart from what my ears have picked up from social discussions, I have personally witnessed scenes of shabby treatment of servants by their masters. For example, with my very eyes I saw a small daughter of a shark in Karko in the north hurling a kettle steaming with hot water at their footman and raining abuses on him as to why he should add Lipton into the water when he knew she only takes coffee. Her mother sat watching them amused, then said, 'Delli my dear, why are you always flying off the handle? Why don't you tell him to heat another water for you?'' Mind you, this man is old enough to born not only this little imp, but her mother as well. With his body sweltering and his clothes bedraggled, he went into the kitchen to heat another water. Now, tell me how a man so abused would have sleepless nights because his masters are dead? Servants to sharks are the slaves of the modern world. As slaves easily rebelled against their masters in the ships and the plantations, servants can be mobilised to rebel against their oppressors. Already poverty has mobilised them. Oppression is like Proteus the Roman god, you know,' he said with more verve than was needed to make his point. 'Oppression keeps changing its form to avoid detection. From slavery to colonialism to globalisation, all is oppression.'

'Whoever bom you, born hare for person,' Biyaku said nodding his head in full understanding of Jokulo's analysis and conclusions, though he spoke in standard English. 'How can I even with my old biabia for face and furu furu for head get good sense like you?'

'This is just a prelude to our strategy, not the strategy, knights,' he said in a stentorian voice. 'Our strategy is that when *we* dispatch a shark to a lonely hell, we bring his servants here to be trained as knights of exorcism. This is our strategy as conceived by me, how do you like it?'

'Quite ingenious,' Haman said, punching the air with his fist. 'Talk of prophets and there you are. What you just told us is a revelation.'

'And when all sharks are swallowed by exorcism, what happens to the Republican government?' Rawka asked.

'It goes with them of course!' Yegama said. 'When a man falls into a well, do you go looking for the trousers he was wearing? The sharks and the government are two dirty sides of the same dirty coin.'

'Fine knights, fine words,' Jokulo went on, grinning from side to side. 'As we are talking here, soon will have men in the north and the east also talking as we are talking and they will strike as we strike. We have come a long way in our anger and plans against the existing despicable system. We have the weapons; our plan is good; our will is unbending. What else do we need? All over the Republic it is going to be a spontaneous and all-consuming insurgency that will not admit as much as a single shot from the enemy. But we need a bond knights. I mean something that would fuse us into one indivisible whole so that we can fight together, win together or die together if need be.

But more important than this, a bond will stop a knight from selling exorcism down the river if we have the misfortune of losing him to the sharks. What do you think?'

'It is not a bad idea in a grave enterprise such as ours,' Rawka asaid.

Barau, Haman, Biyaku and Yegama nodded their assent.

'Then what do you want to be our bond?' Jokulo asked.

'Anything you get for mind,' Biyaku said.

Again, the rest nodded their assent.

'Well, if you are not insisting on your rights as sheriffs of tomorrow's kingdom, I suggest the gun and the dragon be marked on our bodies as the symbol of exorcism and also as our bond.'

'Son of the times!' Yegama cried, saluting Jokulo. 'You are the nemesis of all sharks flashing in the horizon. More than that, you are a royal owl hooting in the dark heralding the coming of a macabre dance.'

'Yegama the gallant knight!' Jokulo cried also saluting Yegama. 'I take your salute.'

After this, it was agreed that each of them be branded on his right thigh with the picture of a rising dragon holding a gun. Jokulo was the first to be branded using a hot knife. Some black powdery substance was applied to the wound everyday. Within days, he was back in the centre of activities in the Shell. After two weeks of his crucification as they called the act of branding, the other five were also branded. When they had all healed, Jokulo admonished them that whatever happened, they should not allow anybody that was not one of them see their thighs where the symbol of their strength and oneness lay. And if any of them should fall into the hands of sharks or the government of the Republic, he should choose to die as a martyr of exorcism rather than betray the struggle. A mere glance at the gun and the dragon or even memory of his agony during crucifixion should toughen such a knight against all forms of torture to make him betray exorcism and tomorrow's kingdom. It was this that stopped Biyaku from telling the police where he was taking the foodstuff to. He considered five years imprisonment nothing compared to betraying the popular hope of millions upon millions of the big extended family of the condemned poor of the Republic. But he could not say this to Ahoka, he being a non-initiate of exorcism.

Later, the act of branding was seen not only as a crucifixion, but also as a baptism into the Shell. The test of knighthood became the courage a man displayed during his branding.

Chapter Twenty-Two

When Jokulo and four of his men came knocking at Okime's residence on the fateful night of the massacre in that house, Ahoka's father was sleeping inside the small cabin by the gate snoring as usual, Jokulo and his men quietly parked their car, a Peugeot 504 station wagon and opened the gate. They saw him sleeping on the long plank inside the small cabin with his mouth wide open. Yegama entered the cabin and stuck the small mouth of his gun into his opened mouth while Jokulo and the other four ran softly to the main house guns in hand.

Solo whose nostrils were half blocked by thick snot and who was breathing largely through his opened mouth, snorted and opened his eyes the moment the gun was stuck into his mouth. When he saw the butt of the gun and the vicious look on Yegama's face, a little urine dropped into his trousers.

'Move as much as your eyelids and I will blow your coconut head to pieces,' Yegama growled at him, two of his front teeth sticking out like the claws of a tiger.

Solo raised his hands pleading for mercy. Yegama removed the nozzle of the gun from his mouth.

'Ogar, please make you no kill me,' he pleaded raising his hands. 'I be poor man with one pikin wey him mama don die. If you kill me, who go helpam for dis wicked Republic?'

'I no go kill you if you do the thing wey I tell you,' Yegama said becoming a little relaxed and in Solo's mind, less vicious.

'Wetin you wan make I do?' Solo asked, relieved of the sudden death that stared him in the face only seconds ago.

'Nothing,' Yegama said, standing up but with the gun still pointing at Solo. 'Just sit down there until I tell you to move.'

Solo sat up his two hands fiddling each other on his thighs.

From the cabin, the two men could hear the breaking of glasses coming from the main house. This was followed by silence.

'Move as much as your eyelids and you will have lead for an early breakfast,' Yegama said his finger curling round the trigger.

'I beg ogar make you no kill me,' Solo sobbed.

'No shooting from me if you behave,' Yegama said.

After about six or seven minutes Yegama said, 'oyah my honourable knight, on our way to the main house.'

Solo stood up and walked out of the cabin to the main house. Yegama followed him behind. They entered the Okimes' sitting-room to find Okime and his family of four lying on their backs. Okime's breath was coming out in short jerks and he was perspiring heavily. His fat face was disfigured by fear. His wife who lay near him was weeping silently into her palms. Their three children lay to her left also crying. The five men stood with their guns leveled at them. The cook a dishevelled looking young man was bouncing on a double executive cushion chair with a beatific expression on his face. In his five years stewardship in the house as cook, this was the first time he had the honour of sitting on a cushion chair in the house.

'Is that their honourable watchman?' Jokulo asked, pointing at Solo as they entered the room.

'Yes, comrade,' Yegama said. 'And who is the chap riding the cushion chair?' he asked Jokulo in turn.

'That is the honourable cook,' Jokulo said, his eyes leaving the Okimes for a moment to stare at the cook. 'Boy, enjoy your ride,' he said. 'As their night of the long knives is here so is your dawn of abundant life.' Then to Solo he said, 'Let the honourable watchman come to me.'

Solo walked to him.

'My honourable watchman, have you passed water this morning?' Jokulo asked Solo. Seeing a confounded expression on Solo's face, he explained, 'I mean to say you don piss for dis morning?'

''No, ogar,' Solo said, wondering why he was asking him such an odd question.

'Please, don't ogar me. There is no ogar for Lucifer Kingdom. Every man na ogar for himself.'

Solo did not say anything.

'Fine, my honourable knight,' Jokulo said his face rippling with excitement. 'Come and piss for dem mouths,' he went on, moving nearer the Okimes.

Solo did not move.

'No be you I dey talk to?' he asked in a quiet deadly voice. The colour of his eyes suddenly changed to that of a cat. He looked wild, vicious and bloodcurdling. Solo felt like fainting. But he moved to stand by the Okimes.

'Now, open your mouths!' Jokulo shouted at the Okimes. They all opened their mouths except Bemi.

'You won't open your mouth?' he blared at her. 'You think I am here to be fucked around by a bitch like you?' he cried, stamping her face with his Italian boots. One of her front teeth flew out to land behind him. As he was stamping her face, he was holding a small round stone in his right hand. The moment he took off his foot from her face, he dropped the stone into her screaming mouth. Her screams were cut off before they could even get to her lips. She started gurgling as he turned to his men.

'You, Rawka remove the whore from my sight,' he said. 'Take her to the toilet and do whatever you feel like with her. Her sight sickens me.' To Solo he said, 'make you begin piss for dem greedy mouths wey chop dem share come chop your own add. If you feel like mess, mess for dem mouths, and if you feel like shit, shit for dem mouths. Mermaid Shell don go burst releasing the gun and the dragon and dem don land for dis house. From here, dem go cast dem net strangling all sharks and whales but leaving eels and scallops to dey swim through its chinks.'

Solo hesitated for only a second before emptying his bladders into the gaping mouths of the Okimes. The urine entered Okime the wrong way and he started coughing holding his neck.

Jokulo kicked him with his boot shouting at him to shut up or be shut up, and for good.

'Good pikin of the kingdom!' he hailed Solo, thumping him on the chest. 'You do well; I dey proud of you. Rawka!' he called Rawka who was still in the toilet with Bemi.

'Yes, comrade!' Rawka shouted back.

'What are you still doing with the slut down there? Do you think we are here to stay till doomsday?'

 'I want to have a bite of her cool, sweet meat comrade,' Rawka shouted back again. 'But the slut is writhing on the floor refusing to catch my line.'

'You know what to do and be here fast,' he shouted wiping away beads of sweat that had gathered on his forehead.

There was a violent struggle in the toilet. A moment later, Rawka came out with a long barbecue knife streaming blood.

Solo's stomach turned when he saw the knife. He quickly looked away. Jokulo was watching him closely to see his reaction. When he saw him looking away, he knew he was scared.

'My dear new knight, make you better start liking things like dis,' he said, his eyes on him. 'Today na the beginning of the dragon's ride through sharks and e go ride far. In future, you no only go see more bloody things like dis, but from your own hands vultures go perch eating human flesh. The thing wey you dey see today na just the tail of the devil.

'So long as you give me gun and allow me go bring my pikin put for Mermaid Shell,' Solo said.

'If na twenty guns you need to fight for tomorrow's kingdom, you go have them. As for your pikin, do you truly loveam?'

'Naim I dey live for.'

'Good. If you loveam as you say you loveam, leaveam where e dey and fight for tomorrow's kingdom wey go freeam from the suffer wey e dey suffer for dis evil Republic. If we allow you go bringam, we don dey show ourselves be dat. Na mystery go help us win dis war. Let gofmen dey wonder who dey kill the sharks: Na the househelps or na some demons wey escape from hell?' Let gofmen no know who e go hunt for. Confusion na our friend for the early part of dis business.'

'I see the sense you dey make,' Solo said, nodding his head.

'Fine,' Jokulo said, turning to Rawka. 'My dear knight, so you want to let off steam. That is not a bad idea. Letting off steam now and then is necessary for the gallantry of a knight. The dish into which you let it off doesn't matter, so long as it goes. So if you can't have the daughter, the mother is as sweet a dish,' he said, smirking at Rawka. 'So go ahead and have your fill.'

Before he could finish talking, Rawka was already out of his trousers moving towards Mrs Okime. The moment she opened her mouth to scream, Jokulo dropped another round stone into her mouth. 'Screaming is forbidden in my kingdom,' he said smiling ruefully at her. 'And may be kicking and gurgling too,' he went on putting the mouth of his rifle on her forehead. 'You gurgle again and the next second you will find yourself on a lonely highway to hell.'

She stopped kicking and lay still like a corpse.

'See what I mean by the powers of gun?' he said, addressing his men. 'With a gun, you are just another Jesus performing miracles at will.' To Rawka he shouted, 'what are you still waiting for?

Rawka who stood shaking like a leaf, flicked away the already loosened wrapper of Mrs Okime, then collapsed on top of her.

'Numbskull, sit up and watch how your sweetie is enjoying the works of her life,' Jokulo said, kicking Okime on his balding head.

He sat up biting his lips and shaking his head.

'Your order is our hunger; we find laughter only in your tears,' Jokulo said, slapping Okime across the face.

A tear, two tears fell off Okime's cheeks as he sat watching Rawka raping his wife, When Rawka was through, the other men had their ways with Mrs Okime in turns. By the time the last man mounted her, she had lost consciousness.

'OK, knights,' Jokulo said, getting up from where he sat watching his men raping Mrs Okime. 'Time is running out. Take the small sharks to their sister in the toilet and be back here under a beat. Then we shall all shrink back together with our new gallant knights into Mermaid Shell.'

With the speed of lightning, Barau, Biyaku, Haman and Yegama descended on Okime's two children and dragged them on their backs into the toilet. Again, there were violent struggles inside the toilet. A moment later, the four men filed out of the toilet each with a barbecue knife streaming blood.

When Okime saw the blood on their knives, he lost all hope of coming out of this cruel show of violence alive. He started violently towards Jokulo, tears bathing his cheeks.

'Fine knights! Fine job!' Jokulo cried, retreating from him. 'The zero hour is here; let the dragon ride!'

Immediately there was explosion of gun-fire snuffing life out of Okime and his wife.

'Knights of the kingdom!' Jokulo cried again; 'back into your shell.'

Chapter Twenty-Three

Inside Jaruwa prison, Biyaku found a fertile ground for the spread of exorcism gospel. His old fears that the coming of the kingdom might suffer a set-back with his incarceration was gone. He was even beginning to see his incarceration as an act of God calculated to take the gospel of exorcism to the condemned sinners of the earth. His disciples were swelling by the day. Within four months of his doing time in prison, almost all the inmates turned adherents of exorcism. If you see two inmates talking and laughing between themselves, you could be sure they were either talking about Jokulo's heroic feats or the coming of tomorrow's kingdom.

Ahoka was Biyaku's first disciple in Jaruwa prison. At first, his reaction to Biyaku's campaign of insurrection was one of anger and bitterness. Why should he be rudely separated from his father for the sake of whatever kingdom, and why should his father be so callous as not to come back home for him? Biyaku told him not to bear his father so big a grudge as he was there when his father requested to be allowed to go and bring him to Mermaid Shell and what Jokulo told his father on that occasion that made him not to come for him.

After many sessions of fiery preaching by Biyaku of the hope that tomorrow's kingdom held for the poor, Ahoka's ill feelings began to wear out until he finally gave in. Together, they started selling the message to other inmates. At a point, it appeared as if he was becoming more fiery and steadfast in his preaching than Biyaku himself. Hardly did he miss an opportunity to speak to a fellow inmate about the joys and wonders of the coming kingdom. In his mind, he saw Jokulo as the messiah of the poor majority; exorcism as the nemesis of all sharks and tomorrow's kingdom as paradise among men on earth. He lived and swore by Jokulo's ideals. The symbol of exorcism and tomorrow's kingdom: the gun and the dragon, which Biyaku had given him after becoming convinced he was as committed to exorcism as any initiate, was never far from him. He spent his time fondling the small picture with the symbol and smiling gleefully to himself. Even when they were taken out to work on the prison farm he had the picture in his pocket. One other thing that occupied his mind was Sindra. He kept wondering what had happened to her since his incarceration. Was she incarcerated like him? From what Mr Binda Kiama told him and his personal encounter with the Republican judiciary, he doubted this. The Great Lafimo would never allow his daughter to be incarcerated like a commoner. All he needed do would be to send a note and some *kola* to the judge and she would go home a free girl. Her sudden and dramatic appearance in the courtroom gun in hand remained an enigma he could not crack. To say he was shocked was to put it mildly. He was thunderstruck. 'What could have made her do it?'

he kept asking himself. As a grown up and a law undergraduate in the university, she could not be ignorant of the penalty for murder or even threatening it. So why did she do what she did; love? May be. Looking at their relationship so far, from their days in Semina Secondary School to date and that flicker of longing he thought he saw in her eyes while they stood under the bridge facing each other, always tried to persuade him she acted out of love. Sweet thoughts of her like this always excited him making him weak. But what future was there for a love relationship between a poor fellow like him and the daughter of the Great Lafimo? he would wonder despairingly. Certainly, the Great Lafimo would never consent to his daughter committing such class suicide as marrying him. 'But wait a minute,' he whispered to himself one evening while thinking of her again inside the prison. 'Tomorrow's kingdom may give fruition to all my hopes. With all the sharks swallowed by exorcism, the Great Lafimo would be nowhere to stand between me and Sindra.' He was excited. 'But, what of Sindra herself?' he reflected further. 'Isn't it possible she too might be swept away by exorcism? Wasn't that what happened to Okime's children?' His heart started beating wildly.

'God forbid bad thing,' he cried silently to himself.

'Wetin dey bite you wey you no fit tell me?' Biyaku who sat watching him asked.

'Make you no mind me,' he said. 'I just dey talk to myself.'

'How I no go mind you my pikin? If I no mind you, who I go mind for dis dirty hole?'

'Fine talk papa,' he said, shifting on his bed where he sat thinking. 'I go tell you wetin dey bite me if you tell me wetin dey wori you dis days wey you dey cough and no dey talk to person.'

For the past three days or so, he had observed a remarkable change in Biyaku's manner of walking and talking. There was a faint limp in his walk, which was not there before and he seldom talked even about tomorrow's kingdom. When he talked, he would run into a hacking cough that left him clasping at his chest.

'I no dey well at all my pikin,' Biyaku said. 'You know I go be sixty-three years? by December dis year. Old man like me, small sickness go fit shakeam.'

'Sori papa,' he said in a voice that carried all the sympathy he felt for the old man. 'Why you no tell me say you no well?'

'No need my pikin. I know say you be small pikin and your wori to dey dis hole dey enough to no let you sleep. How 1 go come add to your wori? Even sef, if I tell you, wetin you go fit do with you barricaded in this hole like ram dem wan bucha?'

'But papa, you for still tell me,' he said, his heart reaching out to him.

'Make you no wori my pikin,' Biyaku said. 'I go soon become fine again. Sickness na natural thing.'

'Which kind sickness dey wori you?'

'The last time I see doctor, e talk say I get tuberculosis or something like dat,' he said. 'You know dis doctors no go tell you your sickness for simple Oyinbo; they must bring big, big Oyinbo dabaru your head. But make you no mind them. Tuberculosis or whatever e callam, man pikin go well again.'

'God forbid bad thing,' Ahoka said with feelings. 'You go live not only to see tomorrow's kingdom but to be gofnor foram.'

'As we don talkam, na so God don talkam, 'Biyaku said. 'God dey see poor man as e dey see rich man. Naim be referee for we obodo Republic. Now make you show me the bedbug wey dey bite you since.'

Ahoka told him about Sindra, their relationship and his fears for her.

'Yes, you get good reason to wori,' he said when Ahoka was through. 'Man no go hate person wey likeam because the person na shark pikin.'

'You see why I dey wori?' he said, sighing.

'Yes, you dey wori for good thing,' Biyaku said again. 'But as we come dey for dis hole how we go fit saveam from exorcism? The only thing to do na to pray make exorcism no reach dem house before we comot here.'

'But, papa, even for your mind you know say dat kind prayer no go work. How many years we go do here? How many sharks Jokulo get to kill before e get to her papa house?'

'But, wetin we go do my pikin as we come dey here wey even to think, dis yeye people wan know wetin you dey think? The thing I go tell you be say, may be dis kind thing na the price you go pay for the coming kingdom be dat,' he said, beginning to cough.

'Papa, me I no go fit pay dis price o,' he cried. 'For Sindra to die, make tomorrow kingdom never come o.'

'My pikin ....,' Biyaku said and trailed away into a hacking cough.

Chapter Twenty-Four

Outside Jaruwa prison, Jokulo and his men continued with their reign of terror. The efficient and ruthless manner of their operation had become a saga in the Republic. North or east, south or west, rich people and their families got wiped out by the day. The print and electronic media were full of their daring exploits. They no longer restricted themselves to butchering the rich in their homes but even on the streets.

After the fall of Biyaku into the hands of the Republican police at the beginning of exorcism, Jokulo felt the bond alone was not enough guarantee that a captured exorcist will not spill the beans under severe torture that dulls the will. So he distributed phials of cyanide to all his men instructing them to always move around with them between their teeth. If any of them was cornered and there was no way out for him, he should crush the cyanide in his teeth and all would be over for him on the instant. That way, he would end up and be celebrated as a martyr of exorcism rather than be scorned as a traitor of the popular hope of the majority poor.

Fear and confusion were grinning at the rich like an ape at the gate of hell. They did not know which was safer: their houses or the streets. But out of habit and human bunker mentality that only the house is safe, they clung to their houses like intent bugs. The streets had become deserted and commercial activities in the busy Strumba Street in Beku city had grounded to a near halt. The sleek, posh cars that cruised around Beku city and other major cities in the Republic had disappeared. What annoyed and terrified the rich was the failure of the police to effect any arrest since the bloodbath began. It was true that a handful of exorcists had been killed. But such exorcists were killed by rich men while defending themselves. None to their knowledge so far had been killed by the police. Rumours circulating within the rich had it that the police had become accomplice to Jokulo and his men so that they always looked the other way while bullets were being pumped into a rich man. This rumour had reached the ears of the President of the Republic making him issue a stem warning to the police. 'Any policeman found aiding, abetting or standing by watching these bandits and subversive elements put the Republic under siege would not only be summarily dismissed from the force, but would also face the criminal process of the land.' This warning was relayed hourly on the national radio of the Republic in Beku. But the rich were not comforted by anything the President said since exorcism began. If anything, his warnings and assurances incensed them to pour abuses on him. In fact, it was reported in one newspaper that one rich man smashed his big colour television to pieces when he could no longer stand the sight of the President appealing for calm among the rich as his administration was doing its best to bring the current madness under control. Now the existence of a club known as *Club de Gallery Human de Vampirists* was no longer a rumour. It was like the dead were rising up in arms against their predators and the predators were forced to confess their sins and seek solace in their heaven beneath the earth: a heaven hitherto said to exist only in the idle imagination of the poor. One rich man by name Okoeduma living in Voro was busy making telephone calls to his fellow rich men in Beku and without to flee into *Club de Gallery Human de Vampirists* as their houses had long become hotbeds. Fleeing to neighbouring countries as political and social fugitives offered a mouth-watering attraction to the embattled sharks. But there again, exorcists were one jump ahead of them. They lay in wait for all sharks pulled out by that attraction along the country's borders, seaports and airports where they despatched them to the great country beyond the clouds for eternal exile.

Within the poor class, Jokulo and his men had become legends talked about in whispers in and outside the Republic. Some of them attributed the inability of the police to nail any of the exorcists to a magical power that made them invisible to the police. Jokulo himself was said to have the powder to disappear when cornered by the police. This sort of talk was common in the evenings in beer parlours. There a drunken man may even swear to having seen Jokulo appear and disappear according to the dictates of his fancy; and another would say he in fact gave Jokulo this magical power that made him invisible. Yet, another man might stand up to demonstrate how he saw a rich man defecating in his trousers when confronted by Jokulo and his men.

When the President of the Republic apprehended his threats to the police were not having the desired effect, he soft-pedalled by promising a handsome reward and promotion to any policeman that would as much as capture a single exorcist. Still there was no result. He then turned to the military the messianic defenders of the Republic. In every broadcast of his appeal to them, he was shown on television with a drawn face and deep sunken eyes asking every military man and woman to rise in defence of the Republic that had fallen under a rule of terror. Above all, he would appeal to their *esprit de corps*. He was a former soldier and the military was his immediate constituency. The military should therefore not allow one of its own to be disgraced out of power by a bunch of bloody civilians. Wherever he went, he was surrounded by hard bitten and trigger-happy young men known as the National Guard for the Survival of the Presidency.

But a big crack had developed within the military hierarchy. High ranking officers being beneficiaries of the President's leadership philosophy of settling potential trouble-makers with large sums of money or political appointment were all for the President's appeal. But the rank and file who had not been settled could not be bothered whether a former military man was disgraced or honoured out of power. Of immediate worry to them was how to feed and clothe themselves and their families in a Republic a packet of sugar went for two hundred rida and a second-class cloth drew as much as a thousand rida. In fact, in Kwanga in the east, two soldiers guarding the house of a retired army officer shot their master and his family dead to make it appear as the handiwork of exorcists, and made away with his property. With the rank and file who constituted the bulk of the Republican military becoming nonchalant and even secret partakers in exorcism, the President and high-ranking military and police officers found themselves in a mud pit inside which they were helpless. The fact that most military officers had developed paunches that made nonsense of whatever military training they had received did not help matters.

So Jokulo and his men continued their reign of terror bumping off the rich to the delight and patronage of the poor.

Chapter Twenty-Five

But inside Mermaid Shell, discontent and ill-feelings were beginning to brew in the minds of Jokulo's disciples. The cause of these feelings was Jokulo's style of leadership, which was beginning to smack of arrogance and repression. At the beginning of the convergence in Mermaid Shell, matters affecting their lives in the Shell or a course of action to be pursued in respect of exorcism were always presented before the assembly of exorcists for deliberation. If at the end of the deliberation a consensus could not be obtained, the matter was put to vote with the will of the majority prevailing. An instance of this was the debate on whether they should start carting away the property of slain sharks or continue with the policy of,' the shark is evil: kill him; his property is rotten: don't touch it.' The debate was prompted by acute food shortage in the Shell with the arrival of new men every day. There was a division of opinion. Hardline exorcists stuck to the policy while liberals called for its suspension or modification to meet present realities,

According to the hardliners, this policy was predicated on the need for exorcists to shun materialism and voracious acquisition of wealth, which were the bane of the Republic they were revolting against. Abandoning the policy would mean a gradual slide into the morass of corruption and economic exploitation of the weak by the strong – both evil manifestations of sharkism. But the liberals argued that the policy was a death-sentence to the extent that it did not put forward an alternative means of feeding the mass of knights increasing by the day. They contended that a rigid adherence to the policy would not only cripple but frustrate exorcism as a man could not be expected to be gallant on an empty stomach. They submitted that for now the policy should be suspended or at least modified to meet present realities. Later, after the triumph of exorcism, it could be recalled. As a matter of fact, the policy would be overtaken by the arrival of tomorrow's kingdom as there would be no shark to kill or his property to avoid, opponents of the policy pointed out. What was more, it was discovered that after killing a rich man and his household and withdrawing back to Mermaid Shell without touching his things, the following morning it would be reported in the print and electronic media that such rich man and his family had been bumped off and his property carted away by the assassins. This became a source of concern, bewilderment and even distrust among the exorcists. Who were the devils spiriting away the property of slain sharks while they were taking the rap or were there Achans amongst them? Opponents of the policy pointed out that if they now resort to making away with the belongings of slain sharks, all these riddles and their threats to exorcism would be solved with a single stroke. After a protracted debate in which Jokulo acted as umpire, it was finally agreed by all that the policy should be suspended if only to further the cause of exorcism. This was communicated to all locations of exorcists in the Republic for implementation.

It was this kind of leadership by mass participation that made all exorcists see Jokulo not only as a grand master strategist, but also as a democrat. But with the passage of time, he turned into a smart Alec seeing himself as something slightly above human not meant to always stoop seeking human opinions. With this feeling came arrogance and repression where dissent was expressed. Though his co-exorcists were largely to blame for his degeneration into a despotic and imperious leader. All that he did or said was always right in their eyes. When somebody tried to express a contrary view, he was shouted down as being ignorant of the philosophy and principles of exorcism and tomorrow's kingdom. But as he began to assume more airs and graces, many exorcists began to resent his style of leadership. Chief among exorcists opposed to his think-nothing-of attitude to ideas of fellow exorcists, were his two bosom friends: Barau and Yegama. The current of resentment and disenchantment came to the surface the day Jokulo said henceforth he would be driven in a siren screaming car wherever he was going. Barau said he was not comfortable with the idea as time was not ripe for such brandishing of power. 'Whoever heard of a thief trumpeting around town?' he asked.

Everybody shouted, 'Barau you have seen it and said it as it is; we start sirening now, we start aborting exorcism.'

'Barau, are you saying I am thief?' Jokulo asked, a sinister expression creeping into his face.

'What's the difference?' Barau hurled at him.

'Well, if I am a thief, so are you and everyone here,' Jokulo said, waving his hand about in an uncoordinated manner. 'What am I saying? Who am I saying it to?' he went on talking down at them. 'I was not seeking your opinions. I was only saying what would be done.' Saying this, he walked away from them into a Lincoln Navigator and drove away with a high pitch siren rending the air.

From this day, his popularity started plummuting dangerously, and with it, perhaps the fortunes of exorcism and morrow's kingdom too.

Chapter Twenty-Six

Something lamentable and choleric depending on which side one's sympathy lay had been happening since exorcism began. It was the sort of thing that would make a dog vomit out of nausea; the sort of thing that hawked the Republic as a rotten commodity among the comity of nations. When this thing could no longer happen because of exorcists' decision to start carting away the property of slain sharks, exorcists and the police clashed in Beku city in the house of one rich man named Teluma who was the man marked for execution that night. After wiping out the man and his family, exorcists took their time removing his household effects into their pick-up vans and *luke-tuke* buses. Then the police arrived catching them on the hop.

Unknown to Jokulo and his men, the police in Beku knew their hideout long ago and had always tailed them to the houses of the rich that had so far been massacred, with the exception of Okime and other sharks butchered at the beginning of exorcism. After tailing them to the house of their victim, they would find a safe hideout some reasonable distance away from the house and lay in waiting. Immediately the exorcists finished their operation and left without touching anything, they would move in and clean out the house; then run to their own hideout in Ardakawa forest. If there was cash, they would share it there and then among themselves and store away the tangible property until the end of exorcism when they would decide on what to do with them: either to sell them and share the proceeds or allocate them among themselves. They so perfected their network of operation that they started operating in shifts for the purpose of fair distribution of what they saw as the windfall of the massacre. There was no time in the day or night that they did not have one of them lurking in the forest surrounding Riakere rocks to keep tabs on happenings in the Shell and the exorcists' next move. When the President of the Republic started issuing threats and appeals.to them, they just laughed and went on with their looting. 'Who cares for any fucking promotion or reward when there are millions upon millions of rida to be made from the wealth studded mansions of the rich,' they said. 'Who is even sure of the said promotion or reward?'

However, this conspiracy was only among the lower cadre of the police force. Most of the senior officers who themselves were targets of exorcism had been killed by the exorcists. The surviving senior officers out of fear for their lives mostly sat in their offices guarded by junior officers. These senior officers were completely in the dark of the conspiracy of the junior officers to feed fat on exorcism. All they heard from their subordinates were loads and catalogues of assurances that they were up to their ears in the hunt for the criminals. It was the common understanding of the lower cadre that after they had benefited to the fullest from exorcism, they would move in and hand over Jokulo and his men to the appropriate authorities.

However, as the fire of exorcism raged on and its windfall multiplied with every operation, they began to have bigger ideas. Those who initially thought of making a few thousand rida from their looting, started thinking of making millions, and those who thought of making millions, started dreaming of becoming multi-millionaires and billionaires. With this kind of money, they would happily put in their retirement letters and repair to their sumptuous mansions to enjoy their loot. So, as the exorcists went on bumping off the rich leaving the spoils behind for them, their appetite for wealth and more wealth sharpened and the D-day for the showdown kept moving forward. What was more, some of them began to fear the exorcists who were gathering strength and fury everyday. The baby monster they could have nipped yesterday had metamorphosed into a ferocious bugbear giving them horrors. 'But then there is the military,' they would console themselves. 'When the chips are down, we can always solicit for their assistance.' But events were later to take a sorrowful and galling twist forcing them to act before they were ready.

As they were chopping and changing their minds on when to halt their looting and move in on the exorcists, the exorcists unwittingly were debating on whether or not to halt their looting by making away with the spoils of their sweat and blood. When they started whisking the properties of fallen sharks, the police went haywire. On the first night of the exorcists' execution of their new policy, they moved in as usual after the exorcists had left to find the house virtually swept. They were enraged. 'What funny pranks are these desperadoes onto or have they gotten wise to us?' they fumed. Feeling sore and down in the mouth, they walked away hoping the disappointing outing they had that night was an isolated misfortune and not a veer by the exorcists from something convenient and beneficial to something despicable and disappointing. But when they continued to meet empty houses for two weeks running, it dawned on them there was a definite change of attitude by the exorcists and that they might as well forget their wild dreams of making it to the exclusive clubs of millionaires and billionaires and make do with what they had gotten so far. Then the crack down, they consoled themselves. Time was more than ripe for it. Though it was very clear to them that they alone might not be able to successfully take on the exorcists given the poor state of their weapons compared to the sophisticated arms of the exorcists, out of a vengeful spirit and a personal desire to vent their anger and frustration on Jokulo and his men, they took them on and in a hit or miss attack. The result was a bloody face off in which the police lost more than a hundred men. When Jokulo and his men later withdrew into Mermaid Shell, a mournful atmosphere hung over Beku and the stench of death filled the air.

But the days of exorcists' solitary sojourn in Mermaid Shell had ran their full course. They had hardly sat down to review the bloody encounter, when the police, the soldiers came storming to Mermaid Shell.

'Let the dragon check!' Jokulo cried the code of taking positions against an enemy.

All exorcists took their strategic positions according to the war plan drawn by Jokulo and other military strategists such as Ahoka's father. The hot war between the government of the Republic and the exorcists was about to begin.

Chapter Twenty-Seven

As the war for tomorrow's kingdom raged in Beku city, Jokulo and a handful of exorcists went abroad on a whispering campaign, wiping up sympathy and support for exorcism among the peasants in the countryside with powerful and moving speeches of the need for them to rally round the exorcists for the total extermination of the minority rich who had for decades held them in poverty and squalor.Whichever locality they visited, Jokulo made sure he had on his entourage a local man who could render his message to his people in their native language. His message to all was the abundant good and joys of tomorrow's kingdom for all irrespective of tribe or religious confession. As for the ills and evils of sharks and their Republic, it was not for him to speak against them as they told their own sordid and cruel tale on their beggarly living standards and conditions.

'How many of you have cars?' he would cry in a farming settlement they had visited.

'None! None!' the villagers who had gathered to hear him would shout.

Yet you spend all your lives eking food from an impoverished soil denied fertilizer by a cruel and inhuman government to feed this nation.'

'Dem don make us suffer heads finish,' they would moan.

'Granted cars are luxuries meant only for sharks as they would like to have us believe; how many of you can feed yourselves decently?' he would ask in a low, soft. beseeching tone, searching their faces.

'None! None!'

'Yet you are supposed to be living in the barn of Africa.'

'Na themselves dem dey fool, no be we.'

'Men do not eat peace; they eat food. Those who want peace must give food to the hyenas of the stomach.'

'True talk!' The people would shout,

'The Republican police were sent to arrest armed robbers but did not return. It was later learned they had joined the armed robbers. Eventually, both the police and the armed robbers were brought to the judges for trial, but the judges joined them. This is the order of things in our Republic today.'

'Death to the judges! Vultures for their judgments!'

'How many of you can give qualitative education to your children?' he would ask in yet another rural community.

'None!' the country folk would cry.

'Yet you are supposed to be breeding the leaders of tomorrow's Republic,' he would say again in a low, beseeching tone.

'Lie! Lie!' they would chorus.

'How many of you live in decent houses?'

'None! None!'

Yet you are supposed to be living in the giant and hope of Africa.'

'Stupid talk, yeye talk, na God go punish them all!'

'Now against your poverty and squalor, raise your eyes and behold the abundance and comfort of fellow citizens like you; working much less than you but feeding much more than you; fewer much more than you but favoured much more than you by a criminal and despicable system!' he would cry, holding up big posters of rich men dining and wining in expensive and exclusive hotels.

Some of the most incensed peasants would jump up, seize the posters from him and tore them to pieces chanting: 'Down with sharks! Down with dem Republic! To hell with sharks! To hell with dem Republic!'

With these kind of firebrand speeches, the countryside was electrified with the fire of exorcism sending fear down the spines of the surviving rich within the Republic and even beyond. With their bows and arrows, machetes and cutlasses, the poor of the Republic began a slow but determined march towards Beku city and other neighbouring cities.

These were the happenings in Beku city and the west. In other parts of the Republic, however, exorcists were still in guerilla warfare with the rich. Jokulo apprehended that unless they come out and engage in an open combat, the government will descend the whole might of the Republican army on exorcists in Beku and emasculate them. To prevent this happening, he left Beku the womb of exorcism to all locations of exorcists in the Republic equipping them with more arms and instructing them to move out and engage the sharks and the government in a total war. This, he reasoned, would force the Republican government to fight all of them at the same time and by so doing, deny it the advantage of concentrating its might on one location of exorcists at a time.

Before Jokulo could return to Beku city after going round all exorcists' locations in the Republic, the whole Republic was engulfed in the most bitter, ferocious and bloody warfare in human history.

Chapter Twenty-Eight

Ahoka was roused up one biting morning by the chanting of a boisterious crowd outside the prison yard. Since the death of Biyaku four days ago, he had never slept well. The slightest sound made him jump. Sometimes he dreamed he was talking with Biyaku about the coming of tomorrow's kingdom when Biyaku would suddenly turn into a leopard and jump at him. He would jump up screaming and sweating.

The death of Biyaku took all the inmates in Jaruwa prison by surprise. On the day of his death, he was his usual self, talking about exorcism and tomorrow's kingdom with fellow inmates. Since he began preaching the gospel of exorcism, he became a celebrity every inmate loved to know and be associated with. No wonder after his death a chilling silence descended on the prison to the disquiet of prison officials. After all inmates returned from the prison farm on the day of his death, he complained to Ahoka his closest ally in the prison of a rumbling stomach and slight fever. Before nightfall, the fever moved from slight to high. Ahoka complained to one of the prison officials about his deteriorating health, but the man angrily asked him if he wanted him to manufacture drugs with his anus to treat ailing inmates. So Biyaku went on shivering with acute fever while Ahoka looked on helplessly. By exactly 9 o'clock pm, he died. Ahoka started screaming and raining curses on all the prison officials. The body was removed from the cell around 10.15 pm and dumped in a shallow grave at the prison's cemetery.

Of all the inmates in Jaruwa, nobody was as bereaved by Biyaku's death as Ahoka. While he was to other inmates a mere symbol of exorcism, he was to him also a father and companion. Day and night, he sat in his cell mourning the death of the man who gave him hope and company in the house of grief and despair. So when he heard chanting and jubilation that cold morning, he nearly jumped out of his skin.

Other inmates also heard the commotion going on outside the prison and started scrambling to their feet to know what was happening. For a moment, the whole prison was turned into a maelstrom by the clattering of eating utensils, tumbling beds and buckets as each inmate struggled to know what was amiss.

The first words that Ahoka could make out of the thundering noise outside sent his heart thumping wildly, fear and happiness gripping him.

'Tomorrow's kingdom is now Lucifer's kingdom!' he heard a man cry out in a microphone. 'Exorcism has swallowed all sharks! The President has fled into exile. The rule of the gun is here!'

He dropped down on his buttocks, too weak to stand. 'All sharks have been swallowed up,' he sighed. 'Poor Sindra, poor me.' Hot tears came cascading down his cheeks.

Outside the prison, Jokulo and his men were tearing one gate after another, advancing into the inner prison. As they penetrated the prison, the man with the microphone kept saying, 'Lucifer's kingdom to the poor, vultures for the sharks; abundant life for the poor, abundant decay for the sharks. Sheriffs of Jaruwa prison, arise and live forever!'

Ahoka was still sitting on the floor weeping when he saw Sindra, gun in hand moving to the other end of the prison. Even in her ruffled military gear, she looked smashing enough to stir the heart of any man. For a moment, it was as if they were back in the courtroom with Sindra pointing a gun at the judge while he looked on stunned speechless.

'Sindra!' he cried, jumping up and waving his hands excitedly. She heard and recognised his voice and spun round. 'Ahoka!' she cried, running to him. By his cell, her frantic hands could not open the cell door.

'Don't suffer your frail hands young lady,' a huge, high-falutting man said from behind her. 'My hands are better at yanking doors than at anything.' With one violent pull he yanked the door open.

Sindra ran in and collapsed on Ahoka.

'Noble sheriffs, salute to the gun and the dragon,' the man said moving further into the prison. 'If baboon must eat now, he must eat by the sweat of his brow.'

For a long moment, Ahoka and Sindra said nothing as they clung to each other shedding tears of joy. 'Sindra,' Ahoka whispered at last.

'Ahoka,' she whispered back.

'How did you join the fight for Lucifer's kingdom?' he murmured.

'For now, leave that to the march of time,' she said, gradually pulling herself away from him. 'Forever let me remove shackles from your unfortunate life.' She made a show of removing handcuffs that were not on his hands and stepped back to give him a beaming smile, before running into his arms sobbing with joy.

Ahoka sobbed with her.

After about two full minutes of being in each other's arms, they pulled apart, but still stood facing each other inside the cell. Then Sindra said. 'My dear Ahoka, you want to know how I became a knight and an exorcist? Don't worry, I will tell you. But first, look at the crucifix with which I was baptised into Mermaid Shell.' She exposed her thigh for him to see the picture of the gun and the dragon branded on her. Ahoka was horrified when he saw the ugly marks drawn on her thigh as a dragon holding a gun.

'But, they don't have to brand women as well,' he said in shock.

'How do you know about the crucifix?' she asked, surprised.

'Biyaku told me.'

'Who is Biyaku?'

'Don't worry I will tell you about him later. Please, tell me how you became a knight and where are your parents?'

'My parents have gone their way as I have gone mine,' she began in a melancholic voice. 'After all, so our lord and saviour prophesied many years ago. Father will turn against daughter and daughter against father and they will go their separate ways.'

'Sindra the prophetess,' he interposed sorrowfully 'You will never change.'

'We change concerning the world but never concerning the word,' she said. 'You see my father would never understand. When Jokulo began the crusade for the coming of Lucifer's kingdom, every rich man took him serious, but my father. To him, the whole thing was a midday madness that would return to sanity by evening. But that was not to be. More and more rich people were being wiped out by the day from north to east and from south to west. But my father like a man doomed by his own fate could only see the exorcists as the scum of the Republic who can only bubble for a while then die of their own contradiction without any positive force being dealt on them. But Jokulo and his men refused to die. Instead, they were gathering strength and fury by the hour. Then my father moved from calling them scum to calling them rebels. But how can the few surviving rich rightly refer to the mass of the Republic as rebels in the mess we found ourselves? I asked him. Change was in the air we breathed, on the streets we trod and the thoughts we thought. 'So who is the rebel? The mass of people fighting for change or the few rich resisting them?' But he would hear none of my words. So when Jokulo and his men came calling at our house, they met him still spitting fire and anger. I lay prostrate at the feet of Jokulo and his men begging to be spared together with my parents and we will in turn become knights of tomorrow's kingdom. But Jokulo said there would be no repentant shark and ordered the dragon to ride on us. But one of his men called Barau said we should not be shot as they were not so much after blood letting as knights for the kingdom. All the men with Jokulo agreed with him except Jokulo himself who started calling Barau a false knight that should go along with us. But the other exorcists said we would only be shot over their dead bodies and levelled their guns at him. In frustration and anger, he entered his car and drove away from our house. That was how we were spared and that was how we became knights in Mermaid Shell. But after just a few days of living in Mermaid Shell, my father and mother disappeared and were later found dead near River Kumbo. Before they vanished, my mother tried many times to persuade me to run away with them, but I refused. I will like to tell you that even as the daughter of rich parents, I have never really felt the poor of the Republic were being given a fair deal. This apart, there was the risk of being captured while fleeing. There was also the strong spirit in me to participate in a war that would free you not only from prison, but from the shackles of poverty as well. If I was able to fight for you alone in the courtroom, why shouldn't I join others to fight for your escape from prison and poverty? For that, I remain proud to this day.'

'Sindra,' he said tears on his cheeks. You have the semblance of a shielded flower, but the nimbleness of a desert warrior. Imagine the way you suddenly appeared in court making his lordship urinate in his trousers.'

'Don't mind the rotten man,' she said. 'The fat sergeant's declaration never went beyond the courtroom; you can trust my father.'

'Sindra the Great!' he cried joyfully, taking hold of her hand.

'Let's go outside to see if I can spot my father among the milling crowd,' he said, making to go out of the cell.

'Hold on,' Sindra said, pulling him back. 'I was coming to your father,' she said, looking sorrowful and bitter.

'But, Sindra, you are full of surprises,' he said, gaping at her. 'How did you get to know my father among the multitude of knights in Mermaid Shell?'

'Remember you are a deadspit of your father,' she said. 'You can see why it was not difficult to get to know him?' she went on after a momentary pause. 'That apart, he was a true knight versed in the art of modern warfare. I think he fought the Wajuwan war of salvation, am I right?'

'Absolutely right, go on.'

'Yes, your father was a gallant knight in Mermaid Shell always leading the attack of Jokulo's men. His gallantry made him a celebrity in the Shell. So the very day I was taken to the Shell I knew him not only as a gallant knight but also as your father. But, eight days later, tragedy struck. He was found lying dead half-buried by sand not too far from the Shell.'

'Papa!' Ahoka cried, slumping down.

Chapter Twenty-Nine

'Now don't disappoint me,' Sindra said, dropping down beside him. 'What of me that lost my father and mother the same day? We have come to a time we must forge ahead leaving the dead to bury their dead. We are moving out of Sodom into our Canaan. To look back is to ask for the fate of Lot's wife.'

Sitting on the floor of his cell, he slumped his head in grief. Four days ago, he lost Biyaku his father in prison and now... 'Will you know what killed him?' he asked her in a tearful voice.

'Nobody really knows,' she said. 'But it was rumoured he was strangled by Jokulo because he was becoming too popular a knight for his comfort.'

'Jokulo again? What is he turning into?' Ahoka wailed.

'What am I hearing like a slanging match outside?' Sindra said, jumping up.

Ahoka also jumped up and the two ran out of the prison. In the small forecourt of the prison, Jokulo stood breathing heavily pointing at a thickset man standing three or four metres away from him.

Although Ahoka did not know him, the man he saw matched the picture of the man he had in mind as Jokulo based on his description Biyaku gave him.

'Imagine the swine telling me I am swelling too big for my pants,' he said, puffing hot air through his nostrils. 'As if that is not enough, that besides me are a thousand and one alternative leaders. Imagine the swollen-headed swine! Where was he when I started sticking out my neck for the kingdom?'

'Don't make much of what slugs like him say,' a tall, skinny man with a hungry look said, tapping Jokulo on his shoulder. 'You know some men are like weeds growing on soils not tilled for them.'

'Ventilate your filthy mouth again and you will have bullets for breakfast,' the thickset man said, pointing his gun at the skinny man.

The man stared at the mouth of the gun, his eyes growing round with shock and fear. He took two steps back, his right hand gradually going to his left shoulder on which his rifle hung. His hand did not travel halfway to its destination when the thickset man pulled his trigger. A stream of bullets ripped open the man's belly spilling his bowels on the ground. The man collapsed on his face as the thickset man swung the mouth of his gun on Jokulo.

'Let the dragon ride on all false knights!' Jokulo cried as the two men fired at each other simultaneously. A thick smoke of gun powder enveloped them. When it drifted away, the thickset man lay on his back, dead. Jokulo's shots had gotten him in the chest. Jokulo was on his knees clutching his right arm, which was badly shattered by the man's bullets.

'Let all false sheriffs begin to trouble,' Jokulo groaned, beads of sweat falling off his face. 'Now that the dragon has finished ridding on sharks, it will start riding on them. Let them begin to trouble.'

'A kingdom that began with butchering its own citizens, what is it worth?'Ahoka who had managed to push his way through the crowd to where Jokulo was, stormed at him.

'Another false knight!' Jokulo cried, his voice becoming faint. He was losing a lot of blood, but nobody offered to tie up his shattered arm for him.'Let the dragon crawl,' he groaned the code of capturing an enemy alive. The knight in falsehood at my feet.' Nobody laid his hand on Ahoka. On his own, he walked to Jokulo. Sindra followed him.

'What is the matter with you, young man?' he squinted at Ahoka as if having difficulty with his vision. 'Are your lips speaking for you or for themselves?'

For my father that you killed,' he said, defiantly.

For a moment, something like recognition flashed across Jokulo's face then vanished to be replaced by a look of surprise.'And who was your father?' he asked, drawing in a smouldering breath.

'He was the man without who tomorrow's kingdom wouldn't be today's kingdom,' Sindra said behind Ahoka.

'Who is the Jacob behind you?' Jokulo asked, grinding his teeth against a stab of pain.' Let him stand out. I hate Jacob more than I do Esau.'

Sindra stepped aside and stood in front of him.

'Ah the shark bitch!' he cried, dissipating his fast-ebbing energy.'So you have turned arse licker? But, even if you are to lick arses, why not lick fresh ones like mine?' He crawled near her and began sniffing her like a piece of meat that was going stale.

Sindra stood looking at him, her lips pouted at a supercilious angle.

'What are you to him?' he asked, pointing at Ahoka with his good hand.

'What is that to you?'

'Everything. Dating gemic ladies with your kind of knockers is my idea of the good life.'

'Different folks, different strokes,' she said, sardonically. 'Seeing mongrels like you is my idea of a horrendous life.'

Jokulo swore and began edging towards his gun lying some metres away from him.

Ahoka picked the gun before he could get to it.

'You should have left him to me,' Sindra said, speaking through her teeth. 'I would have fed the dust with his brain before he lies a finger on it.' The mouth of her gun was centred on Jokulo's head.

'Let the dragon ride,' Jokulo raved, hitting the ground with his good hand.

Nobody paid him attention.

'I say let the dragon ride!' he raved on. 'Are you all deaf?'

Nobody said anything. Then some of the exorcists began laughing and singing:

'Jokulo in a brainstorm

Jokulo in a shellshock.'

'All of you standing here laughing at me will wish you were living under the rule of sharks than in the kingdom!' he cried, slobbering.

'You have said it all!' a man cried at the top of his voice. 'To my mind, it is better to be ridden by fellow men than by dragons.'

'That is the voice of Israel in the wilderness,' Sindra chorused.

The mass of people in the forecourt began to melt away in different directions. Ahoka and sindra followed those going into Beku-city. They had not gone far when they saw a Range Rover coming fast towards them. It came to a storming halt in front of them and two men jumped down. They were also exorcists.

'We have come to warn you,' they said, breathlessly. 'The President has fled to Donku Republic where he had been given troops upon troops of soldiers to come and fight for the restoration of the kingdom into the hands of sharks. So our men must make haste and prepare to defend the kingdom.'

'Which men, which kingdom?' a man asked, sorrowfully. 'There is no kingdom to defend and no men to defend it,' he went on, tears shining in his eyes. 'The linchpin is down there in a brainstorm and the mass of knights have gone their different ways back to dogs' lives.'

'You fool shut up!' another man shouted at the man who just spoke. 'Jokulo has gone off his rockers, so what? There are a million and one leaders in this kingdom that can hold us against the whole world. I, Kursok, son of Rukuwa is one of such leaders and I will lead you not only against the invading sharks, but against the host of heaven and their allies.'

'And I say shut up Moses of Egypt! Who made you leader and king over us?' another man shouted at the latter man, squeezing his trigger at the same time. His gun cracked into life tossing the man into the air. Some other guns cracked into life cutting him out and turning the wtiole place into a wild and violent melee.

'I have always heard my father saying it is not throwing an elephant on the ground that is difficult, but holding and skining it,' Ahoka whispered, mournfully to himself. 'What else can one say about a kingdom that rose and fell at the gate of a prison?'

'I care for no elephants and no kingdom,' Sindra said, excitedly hanging on his shoulder. Her face was transfigured with joy. 'But I care for

civilization and my handsome husband. Ahoka I
love you.'

www.ingramcontent.com/pod-product-compliance
Lightning Source LLC
Chambersburg PA
CBHW020328160726
47992CB00004B/1753